SHADOW OF DOUBT

by

John C. Dalglish

2017

SHADOW OF DOUBT

Get a *FREE* copy of the ebook

"WHERE'S MY SON?"
Detective Jason Strong #1

Visit this link.
http://jcdalglish.webs.com/

OTHER LINKS:

jdalglish7@gmail.com

https://www.facebook.com/DetectiveJasonStrong

John C. Dalglish

Prologue

Rob Layne reacted to the ringing of his shop phone like a man to the sound of a rattlesnake. Recoiling, then approaching cautiously.

"Body Shop."

"It's me, Rob."

As he'd suspected. "Hi, Vanessa."

"Are you not coming home again tonight?"

He glanced at the large, Interstate Battery clock above the garage door. Since it was already 11:00, the answer seemed fairly obvious to him.

"No."

"We have to talk."

"I'm all talked out, Vanessa. I have work to do, and I'm staying here until it's done."

His detective wife was having none of it. "You and I both know that's not the reason you've been sleeping there."

SHADOW OF DOUBT

He'd set up a cot in the office and found it was easier to avoid the nightly confrontations, even though he would have to tell her…eventually. "Come on, Vanessa. It's late. Don't do this now."

"I can't live like this, Rob. We have to get this worked out."

He closed his eyes and rubbed a hand across his weary face, leaving a streak of yellow paint. Catching sight of himself in the office window, he suddenly looked like an Indian warrior, despite feeling more like a coward. "Fine. I'll be home tomorrow night, and we'll talk."

"No. Come home now."

"I can't."

"You can't or won't?"

He hesitated, letting her answer the question for herself. She didn't like it.

"Okay, if you won't come home, I'm coming there."

"No, Vanessa…"

The phone clicked in his ear. He let the handset drop onto its cradle. "Crap."

****

Thirty minutes later, a banging on the metal door stirred him from under the fender of a car. Wiping his hands with a greasy rag, he went over and unlocked the door. Vanessa surged past him.

"Come in." Sliding the bolt closed, Rob turned to find her in a chair that started life as overstuffed but was now severely under-stuffed. She looked back at him through red eyes, her face drawn and tired.

It appeared she was getting less sleep than he was. "Where's Kasen?"

Her gaze dropped to the phone in her hands, watching it as she turned it over and over with nervous tension. "I dropped him at my sister's."

"You shouldn't have gotten him out of bed so late."

"I didn't. I took him over there this afternoon when I thought you might come home finally."

Always tall and thin, she now appeared gaunt. Her normally bright-blue eyes were sunken, and it didn't look as if she'd brushed her hair in days. He was well aware of the impact their relationship issues were having on her, but the impending appeal of her suspension was taking its toll as well.

His heart went out to her. It wasn't that he didn't love her any longer, but the reality was, they'd grown apart. She was married to her job, which had the effect of making him feel like a third wheel. She hadn't found the time to keep the spark alive, and he had given up trying to force it from her.

What spare time she did have was devoted to their son. Despite their problems, she was a great mom. He tried to find the right words.

"Vanessa, I never meant to hurt you."

She didn't look up. "I know."

"It's just not the same between us anymore."

"I know that, too."

"We have to face it. It's time to move on."

She looked up now, her eyes filled with silent pleading. "Why?"

"Why what?"

"Why do we have to move on? Why can't we fight for what we had?"

"Because…"

"Because why?"

He drew in a breath. "Because there's someone else."

She stared back at him unblinking, and appeared as if she was waiting for something. Maybe an invisible hand to flip a switch and reboot her world. A world neither of them recognized, nor could have seen coming just months ago. He took a step toward her.

"I didn't mean for it to happen…"

"How long?"

"Six months or so."

Like a panther, she vaulted from her seat, attacking him wildly. Not like the trained police officer he knew, but a frenzied woman fueled by pain. She pounded on his chest, tears streaming down her face, and cursed at him.

"How could you? You..."

Rob pushed her back and retreated toward the far end of the shop. "Vanessa, calm down!"

She hurled her phone at him, striking his cheek. Ducking into his office, he touched his face, blood coming away on his fingers. Leaning against the office door, he braced for another barrage.

Instead, he heard the front door slam and the sound of an engine roaring to life. The restored 1971 Challenger, the one he'd given her, revved up and sped away into the night. He slid down the door until he was sitting, his body shuddering as his tears began to fall.

****

After relocking the shop door, Rob had laid down, eventually falling into a restless sleep. The sound of the shop's front door

SHADOW OF DOUBT

being tested woke him with a start. His clock read 12:15.

Vanessa must be back for her phone.

He dragged himself out of the cot and flipped on the overhead lights. When he reached the door, he slid open the bolt, then turned and walked back toward the office. He'd not looked for her phone earlier, but found it easily, lying on the ground by the office door.

"I don't want to fight, Vanessa. Looks like you busted the screen…"

He turned and realized she hadn't followed him. Instead, he found himself staring at the end of a gun. Fire blew from the barrel, and hot, searing metal penetrated his chest. Slumping against the wall, Rob was dead before he hit the ground.

John C. Dalglish

Chapter 1

Patty sipped the second cup of coffee she'd had since the start of her shift then rubbed her eyes. Most times, the overnight desk from eleven to seven was relatively busy. With just three of them on duty at the emergency dispatch center, a steady stream of calls would keep them awake and alert.

This night had been the exception, thus coffee number three had come just ninety minutes into the shift. Greg and Misty had gone to the break room for a bite to eat, so the next call came directly to Patty.

"9-1-1, what is your emergency?"

"I need to report a shooting."

"Okay. What is your location?"

"The Layne body shop at 811 Broadway."

"Is the victim alive?"

"No."

"What about the shooter. Do you know where they are?"

SHADOW OF DOUBT

"Gone, I suppose."
"What's your name?"
"Vanessa."
"Okay, Vanessa. Are you hurt?"
"No."
"Are you safe?"
"Yes. I'm in the office."
"Good."

Patty punched the info into the computer. *Shots fired at 811 Broadway. Police and Medical required. One victim, location of shooter unknown.*

"I have police and EMTs on the way."
"Okay."

Patty was surprised at the caller's matter-of-fact monotone. "You're doing great, Vanessa. Stay on the line…"

The line went dead.

****

Vibrating on the bedside table, the phone next to his head pushed an irritating buzz into his sleep. Whether from instinct or just years of practice, he reached over and snatched up the cellphone.

"This is Strong."
"Jason, it's Torres."
"What's up?"

"Lieutenant Savage called. We need to respond to a scene."

Jason pushed himself from under the blankets. "When?"

"Now."

"No, not that. When did he call?"

"I just hung up with him."

Jason rubbed his eyes. "Why do you sound so awake then?"

"I don't know. I guess I just wake up easily."

He grunted. "Well, that makes one of us. I'll pick you up in twenty minutes."

"Good."

He closed the phone and turned to look at Sandy. His wife never slept through a late-night call, and looked up at him through bleary eyes.

"Gotta go?"

"Afraid so." He leaned across the bed and kissed her. "Say good morning to the kids for me."

"I will. Be safe."

Ten minutes later, he was dressed and walking out to his car, a cup of coffee in his hand. The current heatwave smothering South Texas, oppressive during the day, was no less miserable at night. A moonless sky, combined with high humidity and very little breeze, made for a suffocating darkness.

SHADOW OF DOUBT

A case on these kind of nights could be anything, but it was likely the trigger was the heat. More than a few times, he and Vanessa had been called out to a scene where, sparked by drinking and heat-shortened fuses, someone had ended up dead.

With Vanessa on disciplinary leave, Jason was working cases with the newest detective to San Antonio Homicide, Dianna Torres. So far, the partnership had been effective, though a little strained.

Where Vanessa was calm at a scene, evaluating things with a methodical efficiency, Torres was the opposite. Constantly moving, she would talk and think at the same time, sometimes in the wrong order. Nonetheless, they had already worked and solved three cases together.

At just a little past 1:30, he pulled up at her door to find her waiting for him on the front porch. She wore her blonde hair pulled up in a bun, and she had managed to get all her makeup on.

She got in and slammed the door. "Hey, Jason."

"Hi. Where are we headed?"

"811 Broadway. Some sort of car repair joint."

"Okay. Did Savage give you any details?"

"Not much. Single male, gunshot, called in by the person who found him."

Jason looked over at her. "Found him or shot him?"

Torres smiled. "Good question."

****

A lump formed in Jason's chest as they came down Broadway toward the tan brick structure. Located on a downtown street corner, the address was in a part of the city that was mostly deserted at night. As they approached the scene, it seemed the only persons moving about wore uniforms.

He hadn't put the address together with his friend, but as they pulled up, his heart sank. Yellow crime tape surrounded Layne's Body Shop.

"Oh, no."

Torres must have picked up on his tone. "What is it?"

"I know the owner of this shop."

"Who is it?"

"Vanessa's husband."

For a moment, the impossible happened—Torres was speechless. Jason slammed the car into park and jumped out. Running up to the officer on duty, he held out his badge, then ducked under the yellow ribbon. A few more steps and he stood at the open shop door.

A couple of EMTs were just packing up from checking the body, which was now covered by a white sheet, a spreading red stain discoloring the top of it. Jason moved unsteadily toward the victim, fighting the dizziness that threatened to overtake him. Partly to keep from falling down and partly to do what had to be done, he kneeled next to the body.

Drawing in a deep breath, he reached for the edges and pulled the white shroud back from the face. Every detective's worst fear is to find the body of a friend or family member, and Jason had been fortunate enough to avoid it up until now. As a result, nothing could have prepared him for what he saw.

"Oh, no. Oh, Rob."

His eyes filled with tears, and his stomach churned. Sensing he might vomit, he dropped the sheet and turned away. Struggling to gain control, he pushed himself to hone in on the job he had to do; his personal anguish would have to wait for another time.

Focus, Jason! Focus! Where's Van...?

He stood and spun, searching the shop for his longtime partner. The responding officer stood next to Jason, expecting to give his report, but Jason ignored him and went out front. After several frantic moments, he spotted Vanessa talking to Torres.

"Vanessa!"

She turned toward him, and the sight of him must have been too much for her; she lost it.

She took two steps and slumped against him. He put his arms around her and did his best to keep her from collapsing to the pavement.

"I'm so sorry, Vanessa. I can't believe it."

He helped her over to a bench and sat her down. Dried blood covered her hands, as well as a streak on her face where she'd wiped at her tears. He dropped down next to her. "How did you find out?"

"I came back to get my phone, and he was lying there."

"*You* found him?"

She nodded. "I checked his pulse, but he was gone."

Torres had followed them to the bench. "Did you see anyone else?"

"No. I pulled up, and the door was open. Of course, I cleared the shop before checking on Rob."

"What about other vehicles?"

Jason scowled up at his current partner. "Perhaps you could get the responding officer's report before we ask any more questions?"

Dianna hesitated then nodded. "Of course."

When she was gone, Jason turned back to Vanessa.

"Where's Kasen?"

"He's with my sister. I dropped him off this afternoon."

As the coroner's van pulled up, Jason realized the sensitivity of their position. The death of an officer's spouse is the kind of case that had to be handled with tremendous care. He looked down at Vanessa.

"Are you okay for a few minutes?"

"I think."

"Good. Stay here."

Jason rose and walked over to where the coroner's assistant was unloading a gurney. "Hold off on that."

The young man turned, surprise on his face. "Okay…what's up?"

Jason showed his badge. "I'll need to take some special measures for this scene. Wait until you get orders from your boss, okay?"

"I guess."

Jason pulled out his phone and dialed Savage.

"This is Savage." He was apparently still awake from calling Torres earlier.

"Morning, Lieutenant. This is Jason."

"What have you got?"

"Well... It's a delicate situation, and I would like your input."

"Okay, shoot."

"Torres and I have identified the victim at our crime scene. His name is Rob Layne."

"Layne? As in Vanessa Layne?"

Jason sighed. "Yes, sir. It's her husband."

"Dear Lord. Is she there?"

"Yes sir. She found the body."

Several moments of silence passed, and when the lieutenant next spoke, his tone had changed. "Do the following. First, do not let her near the scene again. We have to protect the investigation from any appearance of sloppiness or favoritism."

Jason didn't like the insinuation but held his opinion. "Very well."

"Second, do not let any coroner representatives nor forensic personnel into the scene. I'll be in touch with both Doc Davis and Doc Josie; they'll determine who they want to process the evidence."

"I understand."

"Finally, let Torres take the statement from Detective Layne. Am I clear?"

This time, Jason wasn't about to remain silent. "But, sir, I can do—"

SHADOW OF DOUBT

"What you can do is what I tell you! Is that clear, Detective?"

"Yes, sir"

"Good. I'm on my way."

The line went dead, and Jason put away his phone. He returned to the bench, but Vanessa was gone. Inside the garage, Torres was talking to the responding officer when Jason tapped her shoulder. "Have you seen Vanessa?"

"Yeah. She's in the office."

Jason's heart jumped into his throat. "Vanessa!"

She stuck her head out the door. "Yeah?"

"I need you out of there, please."

She hesitated, but then a look of understanding came over her face. "Of course."

Jason turned back to Dianna. "Savage has asked that you get a statement from Vanessa. In the meantime, no one touches the scene until he gets here."

"Okay."

Jason raised his voice. "Everyone, listen up! I need all personnel out of the shop immediately. Thank you."

Although there were more than a few confused looks from the techs, they heeded his order and moved toward the exit.

The scene was on lock-down.

John C. Dalglish

****

Though coffee had helped him wake up, Lieutenant Eric Savage was now running on adrenaline. In his time at College Station PD, he'd worked two murders involving members of the department. Those cases did not produce fond memories.

The first was an officer's wife found dead in her home. The officer had claimed to be on patrol, but eventually it was proven he'd gone by the house in his police cruiser. His wife had been having an affair, and his solution had been a permanent separation. The kids were the ones who'd suffered the most.

The second case involved one of Savage's former patrol partners. Her husband had been ambushed, and though she'd been three hundred miles away at a training conference when it happened, her lover turned out to be the shooter. She had been in on the plan from the start.

Both cases had been sensational, but worse, the entire department had been put on trial. He took part in both of those investigations, but this time would be different; this time, he was in charge. He had to get it right.

SHADOW OF DOUBT

Picking up his phone, he made the first call.

****

Captain Sarah Morris had gotten used to sleeping through the night. As head of the Major Crimes Division, she had been able to recruit and place strong leaders under her. As a result, she was rarely bothered at home with a situation beyond the control of her lieutenants. A fact her new husband Gavin appreciated.

For that reason, the phone rang five or six times before bringing her out of a deep sleep.

"Hello?"

"Captain Banks?"

"Yeah...Yes. Who's this?"

"Lieutenant Savage."

Sarah pushed herself up on one elbow. "What is it, Eric?"

"Vanessa Layne's husband was murdered earlier this evening."

"Dear Lord! Is Vanessa okay?"

"She's fine, but there's a problem."

"A problem? You mean besides the murder?"

"Yes, ma'am. Detective Layne was the one who found the body."

Sarah hesitated then asked, "Was anyone else with her?"

"No."

Wrong answer, Eric.

"Okay, you handle the scene. Get Doc Davis and Doc Josie to respond personally. I'll call the chief."

"Very well."

"And Eric…"

"Ma'am?"

"Every *I* dotted, every *T* crossed. Clear?"

"Clear."

Sarah hung up and slid out of bed.

Gavin rolled over and said something, but she didn't hear him. She was already in the bathroom, getting dressed.

****

One of the perks of being Chief Medical Examiner was that Dr. Leonard Davis rarely had his nights interrupted by work. Of course, the reason he wasn't called at home might have been because he didn't take kindly to it. He snatched the ringing phone off the cradle.

"Yeah!"

"Doc?"

"Yeah. Who's this?"

"Eric Savage."

Doc lay on his side, head still on the pillow and the handset to his ear. "Who?"

"*Lieutenant* Savage."

Doc had never received a call at home from the new lieutenant. He sat up, adrenaline kick-starting his brain. "Yes, Lieutenant. What's up?"

"We've got a situation that requires me to ask you to personally respond to a scene."

"What sort of a situation?"

"Detective Vanessa Layne's husband was murdered earlier this evening."

Doc struggled to catch up. "Our Vanessa?"

"Yes."

Pictures, like a slideshow behind his eyes, slid across his consciousness. Vanessa, Rob, Kasen, Jason. Now one of those people was dead and the others struggling with unimaginable loss. Doc stood, phone still to his ear, and began to dress.

"Where?"

"811 Broadway."

"I'm on my way."

****

Dr. Jocelyn Carter had always struggled with sleep. Ever since her days at college, where being awake late into the night to study was an asset, she'd never been able to sleep for more than four or five hours at a time. She often found herself sitting at the kitchen table with some orange juice and a book, reading until her eyelids drooped enough to warrant another try at sleeping.

This was where she found herself when the ringing phone split the early morning quiet. After giving her heart a few seconds to resume beating, she picked up the call.

"Hello?"

"Doc Josie?"

"Yes."

"This is Eric Savage."

"Good morning, Lieutenant. This is a surprise."

"I'm sure. I'm sorry to get you up, but I need your help."

"Okay. What's the problem?"

"You're familiar with Vanessa Layne's husband, Rob?"

For the second time in less than a minute, her heart skipped a beat. "Of course."

"He was murdered last night."

"Murdered! What about Vanessa? Is she okay?"

"That's why I called you."

"Was she hurt?"

SHADOW OF DOUBT

The lieutenant sighed. "She's not injured…but she was the one who found the body and called it in."

Nausea flowed over her as the implications rolled around in her head. "What do you need from me?"

"I want our best on task."

"What's the address?"

"811 Broadway."

"I'll be there in half an hour."

****

For William Murray, a late-night phone call led to panic of a different sort. Because he rarely heard from work at that hour, the ringing prompted immediate concern for his two daughters. Both were away at college, and he worried about them just about all the time, although he knew better. They were more than capable of taking care of themselves.

He picked up his bedside phone before the second ring.

"Hello?"

"Chief?"

Being called by his title gave him a moment of relief; his girls were fine. However, that feeling was quickly replaced by one of uneasiness. "Yes. Who's this?"

"Captain Morris."

"Yes, Sarah. What can I do for you?"

"We have a bit of a situation, and I felt it best to make you aware."

"Very well."

"One of our people, Detective Vanessa Layne, discovered her husband murdered last night."

"That's awful. Did you say *she* discovered him?"

"Yes, sir."

Murray ran his hand through his hair, squeezed his eyes closed, and pushed himself to think. "What steps have you taken to insure the integrity of the investigation?"

"Lieutenant Savage is handling the scene, and he's contacting the heads of both forensics and the medical examiner's office. They should be responding, as well."

Something was scratching at the back of his brain. "Layne? Isn't she on suspension for hitting a suspect?"

"Yes, sir."

He groaned. "Keep me advised."

"Yes, sir."

SHADOW OF DOUBT

Chapter 2

While the interior of the garage was in a kind of frozen stasis, the outside of the building had become a manic combination of flashing lights, yellow tape, and gawking spectators who had come from Jason knew not where. Officers stood in groups of three or four, talking under their breath; it seemed the whole department was at the scene.

Jason spotted the lieutenant's black sedan as it came to a stop. Walking over to where Savage was approaching the yellow-tape perimeter, Jason marveled at how his boss always looked the same, whether it was midday or midnight. The olive skin of his head and face was clean-shaven, and his demeanor was one of control. Nevertheless, intensity and passion fueled the man, but Savage never let those emotions show on his face.

"Hi, Lieutenant."
"Hey, Jason. What's the status?"

"Scene is locked down. Vanessa is sitting on a bench outside the shop."

"Okay. I called both Doc Davis and Doc Josie and asked them to respond personally. They should be here anytime."

Torres walked up. "Hey, Lieutenant."

Savage nodded. "Do we have a preliminary statement, Dianna?"

"We do."

"How does it look?"

"Plausible but filled with problems."

"What about evidence?"

She pulled out her notepad. "Not much so far. The victim appeared to have a single gunshot wound to the chest, but I'm still waiting on the coroner for more info. We had just started looking for bullet casings when Jason shut things down."

"Good." Savage looked around at the large number of officers. "We've got more than enough manpower here. Let's put them to use. Get a neighborhood canvas going, and make sure they cover both this street and the one that runs behind the shop."

"Yes, sir." Torres turned and left.

Savage pointed toward the garage. "Come on, Jason. Show me what we've got."

Inside the shop, the lack of a breeze made the space stifling, and sweat glistened on his boss's scalp. Jason couldn't be sure whether it was from the heat or the stress. Probably both.

Pointing from where they stood just inside the front door, Jason briefed the lieutenant.

"Shot seemed to come from this direction. There are no obvious signs of forced entry, so either the door was unlocked, or Rob let the shooter in."

Savage scanned area. "Were you able to determine if anything was taken?"

"Not yet. Unfortunately, the best person to determine that is Vanessa."

"Okay. After the scene is fully processed, bring her back in for a look around, but she doesn't touch anything. I don't want her altering the scene."

"Yes sir, but you don't suspect her, do you?"

"It's not about that; it's about making sure we do everything by the book. No shortcuts, understand?"

"Perfectly."

"Have we seen any press yet?"

Jason shook his head. "Not to my knowledge."

"Well, it won't be long."

"Morning, gentlemen."

Jason and his boss turned to see Doc Davis, his large form filling the doorway as he walked in, a bleak expression giving evidence to his distaste for the work ahead of him.

Savage nodded at the big coroner. "Hey, Doc. Thanks for coming so quickly."

"Of course."

With some effort, Doc crossed the garage, kneeled next to the body, and removed the sheet. This time, Jason saw not only his friend's face but also the wound in his chest.

Doc examined the body for a long time then turned to Jason. "Have photo's been taken?"

"Yes."

Doc turned back and rolled the body partially onto its side. "You see this?"

"What?"

"The pool of blood; it's fairly small."

Jason leaned closer. "What's that tell you?"

"There's a good chance the bullet hit the heart. Pumping stops immediately; less blood leaves the body."

Jason made a note while Doc let the body return to its original position. "Entrance wound is sizable, possibly made by a large-caliber slug."

"Can you estimate time of death?"

"Three or four hours probably."

Jason looked at his watch. 3:15. "Vanessa found him at about 12:30, so that fits."

Doc pushed himself back to his feet. "I want another set of pictures before I remove the body. Then give the word, and I'll transport."

"Okay. I'll check with Doc Josie before you remove the victim."

Torres came in. "Canvas is started, and Doc Josie just pulled up."

Savage nodded. "Where's Detective Layne?"

"This way."

Torres led the small parade back outside to where Vanessa sat on a bench. Her red eyes and absent stare said it all. She didn't look up, even when the lieutenant greeted her, so he touched her shoulder.

"I'm so sorry, Vanessa."

"Thank you, sir."

"I know you've given the basics to Dianna, but I need you to go downtown with her. We have to get a detailed statement while everything is fresh."

A barely perceptible nod. "Of course."

"Thanks." He turned and nodded to Torres. "Who drove?"

"Jason."

"Okay. Put her in my car, and I'll drive you both downtown."

SHADOW OF DOUBT

"Yes, sir." She reached out to help her fellow detective up. "Come on, Vanessa. Let's get this over with."

Jason watched his partner being led away. She looked so small and frail, a picture unlike her in every way. The knot in his chest grew a little larger.

The large letters on Doc Josie's van, CRIME SCENE INVESTIGATIONS, changed from their original white paint to red, then blue, then back to white in a non-stop cycle of rotating police lights.

The two men walked over to the back of the vehicle, where the forensic department head was unloading her equipment. She slammed the door closed and looked up, anxiety obvious in her grim smile. "Morning."

Savage forced his own half-smile. "Thanks for getting here so fast."

"Of course. Show me what you've got."

The lieutenant's cellphone rang, and after looking at the number, he nodded at Jason. "I'll let Strong take you inside while I get this."

Jason turned and headed toward the door, Doc Josie falling in step with him. "How's Vanessa holding up?"

Jason shrugged. "As well as possible, I guess. She's pretty shaken."

"I can imagine. None of us ever wants to find a loved one dead."

"You've got that right, and especially murdered."

They arrived at the door, held open by an officer, and entered into the brightness of the shop. Josie stopped, put down her bag, and surveyed the garage. As she moved methodically from one side to the other, Jason could almost hear the little clicking of her mental camera recording the scene.

Doc Davis came up behind them. "Hey, Josie."

"Hey, Doc. Are you finished?"

"Yeah. I'm ready to transport."

"You get a set of photos?"

The big man nodded, the effort seemingly sapping the last of his energy. "Yes, but primarily of the body."

"Okay. Let me shoot the whole scene with the body still present, then you can pull him."

"Let me know when."

"Okay." She reached into one of her bags, pulled out her camera, and began shooting.

When she'd finished, she looked over to where Jason was standing. "Okay, you can start your search."

While she went to notify Doc Davis he could transport, Jason found some numbered crime scene triangles in her bag and began moving about the shop.

Slowly and deliberately, he hunted for anything relative to the shooting. Using a flashlight, despite the lights being on, he focused on finding a reflection that might be a bullet casing. If he didn't find one, it might indicate a revolver was used.

Near the office wall, not far from the body, he spotted a cracked cellphone. It looked like his partner's, but he couldn't be sure. He placed a triangle next to it.

Moving into the office, Jason scanned the walls for signs of a bullet hole. If the shooter missed his target, Jason hoped he might find a slug where he could retrieve it.

Instead, he found himself looking at photos of Rob, Vanessa, and Kasen during happier times. Car shows, a trip to Galveston Island, going to a Cowboys game, and numerous others spoke about a time when this night could never have been thought possible.

Jason shook his head in an effort to clear his mind and noticed a clean spot where a photo used to hang. He made a note of it before resuming his search.

Robbery could certainly have been a motive, and his search of the corner file cabinet produced an empty bank pouch. He bagged it for evidence, hoping for a fingerprint. Also in the cabinet, he found a ledger with customers' names, addresses, and phone numbers. Next to each was listed a description of the work Rob had performed. Jason took the ledger into evidence.

Scanning the desk, he found little of interest. Pens, auto parts receipts, and an old piston head serving as a paperweight. The side drawers were locked, but when he pulled the center one out, it unlocked them all. The drawers were mostly empty, and the desk appeared to be more of a convenient place to dump stuff than to conduct business.

Moving back out into the garage as Doc Josie returned, Jason stopped by the office door while Josie paused near the front door. He could sense her thinking the same thing he was.

Aside from the body, it was nearly impossible to tell if something was out of place.

Typical of a busy garage, workbenches bore the weight of tools and auto parts, all of which were strewn haphazardly about. Rolling work carts overflowed with rags and wrenches, and almost every wall sported a different color of paint overspray.

Josie nodded toward the yellow triangle near Jason's feet. "Find something?"

"Cellphone. I think it's Vanessa's, but I figured you'd want a photo before I bagged it."

"Indeed. What about bullet casings?"

Jason waved his hands in exasperation at the chaotic mess. "It's almost impossible to find anything that small in this mess."

"Can we narrow down the location of the shooter?"

Jason looked down at his friend's body. "It appears Rob was standing about where I am, looking toward the door. The shooter was probably somewhere between you and me, facing the office."

"Okay. We know most guns eject back and to the right. If it wasn't a revolver, the casing is more likely to be on this side of the room. Let's concentrate there."

Jason flipped on his flashlight and retraced his path toward the entrance, but this time, he did so on his knees, looking under every table and shelf.

Doc Davis came in. "Lieutenant Savage has taken Torres and Vanessa downtown."

Jason nodded but continued his search while the coroner loaded Rob's body onto a gurney. Josie photographed then bagged the cellphone. An eerie silence weighed on the room, born out of a mixture of concentration and grief.

When the gurney rolled by on its way to the door, Doc Davis stopped. "I found this in Rob's pocket."

Jason took the wallet and opened it. Inside were two tens and a twenty-dollar bill. Jason dumped the wallet into an evidence bag. "Hey, Doc, you have a guess where the shooter might have been standing?"

"Well…the shot was to the torso and not to the head. The bullet made a big hole in his chest, but it didn't go through him, and there was no gunpowder stippling around the wound. My guess is the shooter was between five and ten feet away."

Jason stood. "So from the front door to maybe halfway across to the office?"

Doc scanned the distance. "Looks about right."

"Thanks, Doc."

"Sure."

As the gurney finished its trip out into the first light of morning, Jason went to the halfway point indicated by Davis. Moving backward a step at a time, he extended his arms as if firing a gun. After each step, he would glance to his right then kneel down to look where a casing might have landed.

Eventually, he reached the entrance. His turn to the right had him looking directly at the door itself. If he'd had a lightbulb above him, it would have been flashing. Apparently, just the look on his face was enough for Doc Josie.

"What is it?"

Jason held up a hand but didn't answer. He turned and stepped outside, looking down at the ground on the opposite side of the door. Among some gravel, he saw it.

Josie had come to the door. "Find something?"

Kneeling down, he lifted the casing on the top of his pen and turned to show her the piece of brass bobbing uncertainly. "I did. Looks to be a 9 millimeter."

Jason returned it to the gravel and covered it with a yellow marker. "It appears our shooter was standing just inside the door. I reasoned an ejecting shell would hit the door and probably be deflected outside."

She took a couple photos then gave him an evidence bag. "Nice work."

Jason managed a grin. "Thanks. Coming from you, that's a real compliment."

She laughed, breaking some of the tension they were all dealing with. "Don't let it go to your head. I could point out how the exterior of the building should have been searched already."

Jason bagged the casing. "I'll ignore the fact you said that."

"What about vehicles? Are Vanessa's and Rob's cars here?"

Jason pointed toward a pair of vehicles parked off to the side of the shop entrance. "The red, souped-up Mustang is Rob's. Vanessa's Challenger is the one next to it."

"We need to have both cars processed. Can you arrange to have them towed?"

"You got it."

****

When Jason returned to the inside of the garage, he found Doc Josie in one corner of the room, searching and photographing.

"Do you need anything else from me, Doc?"

She looked up. "I've got three more techs coming to help me catalogue everything. So there's just one thing."

"Okay. What?"

"Stay out of the way."

Jason smiled. "Your wish, my command, and all that. I'm gonna go to the station and check on Vanessa."

SHADOW OF DOUBT

Doc Josie gave him a knowing look. "Afraid to leave her alone with Torres?"

Jason grinned. "Something like that, but the other way around."

As he made his way back outside, the sun was just peeking over the horizon. Already making its presence felt, they were obviously in for another scorcher of a day.

He was just about to get into his car when a familiar voice stopped him.

"Jason! Wait up."

He turned to see the muscular frame of Devin James, and Jason had to force himself not to groan out loud. Despite being over sixty, James had the energy and drive of a man half his age, much to the detective's frustration.

"How many times have I told you not to call me Jason?"

Devin dismissed the question with a wave of his hand. "Sorry, sorry. Detective, can you give me a statement?"

The press corps had not shown up in force yet, but James was like a personal plague for Jason, following him around like Pigpen's cloud. "Not at this time."

"Oh, come on. My sources tell me the victim is Rob Layne, your partner's husband."

"What sources are you referring to?"

"You know I can't reveal that."

Jason nodded. "And you know I can't give you any details."

The reporter would not be dissuaded, which was exactly what made him so annoying and good at his job. "What about Vanessa? Was she present? Was she hurt?"

"Vanessa was not hurt."

"She's the spouse. Is she a suspect?"

It had been a long night already, and James was making it longer. Jason leaned in close to the reporter's face, lowering his voice to a hiss. "Don't even think of going there, do you understand?"

Devin took a couple steps back. "Easy, Jason. You and I both know the spouse is always the first to be checked out."

"There's a difference between being checked out and being a suspect. Don't lose sight of that, James."

"So she is being checked out."

Jason didn't try to hide his hostility. "Don't push me, Devin."

He got into his car and slammed the door. The reporter asked another question, but Jason couldn't make out the man's words over the sound of the engine as he drove off.

After taking out his phone, he dialed Sandy.

"Hello?"

"Hey, it's me."

"Jason, you don't sound good. Something wrong?"

She always knew when things were bad. Call it a cop wife's radar. "Yeah. I've got some bad news."

"I can tell. You're scaring me, so out with it."

"Rob Layne is dead."

"Dead… How?"

"He was shot at his garage last night."

"Oh, my. How's Vanessa?"

"Pretty rough. She found him."

Sandy sucked in a deep breath. "That's horrible. Do you know who shot him?"

"No. They're getting a statement from Vanessa now."

"They don't think she did it, do they?"

He hesitated. Even though he knew his partner better than anyone, and he was convinced she wouldn't or couldn't shoot Rob, the lieutenant and others were less likely to give her a pass.

"Jason? Are you there?"

"Yeah. Right now, they're just getting a statement."

"Let me know how things are, okay?"

"I will. Love you."

"Love you, too."

He closed his phone as a sense of foreboding settled on him like the sheet that had covered his friend's body. Ugly things remained hidden until someone came along and lifted it.

He hoped it wouldn't have to be him this time.

SHADOW OF DOUBT

John C. Dalglish

Chapter 3

Vanessa sipped the balance of her coffee from the foam cup, then set it on the table. She'd been in that interview room hundreds of times before but couldn't ever recall sitting in the seat where she now found herself. It struck her as odd how very different things could look just by switching sides.

Instead of a blank wall and a suspect, she found herself facing the large, two-way mirror, and being watched by the video camera mounted near the ceiling. Her mind could recreate the view from the observation room after doing so many interrogations, and she wondered who was watching her. It was unsettling to be in the role of the mouse rather than the cat.

Her mind kept flashing back to the scene at the garage and the panic that had gripped her. Everything she'd counted on had disappeared in an instant, and though she'd wanted to run from it, she couldn't.

SHADOW OF DOUBT

She'd had to check on him, she'd had to make sure there wasn't someone in the garage, and she'd had to call it in. That was the most difficult part of all. It took all the strength she could muster to calm herself and make a 9-1-1 call that could be understood by the operator.

Once she'd completed the task, she'd shut down. Closing off emotionally was a defense tactic she'd learned from too many bloody crime scenes. Cut off the emotions and focus on the task at hand.

People become bodies, animate objects become inanimate, family members become witnesses, and blood becomes evidence. But that wasn't going to work much longer.

Soon, perhaps in the next few hours, or maybe the next few minutes, she would have to face the reality and impact of Rob's death. She was a widow. Kasen had lost his father. Their lives would never be the same again.

While on the way to the precinct, she'd borrowed the lieutenant's phone to call her sister.

"Hello?"
"Hey, Rach. It's me."
"It's early, Vanessa. Is something wrong?"

"I know, and I'm sorry, but I have some bad news."

"What is it, sis?"

"Rob is dead."

Her sister's shock was audible on the phone as she let out a small cry. "What? How?"

"He was at work, and somebody shot him."

"Oh, no. Do I tell Kasen?"

Tears streamed down as she pictured the innocent face of her son. "No. Don't say anything. I'll tell him myself."

"Of course, sis. When will you be here?"

"I'm not sure. There're some things to take care of before I can leave. I'll call you."

"Very well. I'm so sorry, Vanessa."

She brushed at her tears. "Me, too. I gotta go."

Startled, Vanessa jumped when the interview room door opened, pulling her back to the present. Torres came in, her forced smile attempting to mask her tension. As she sat opposite Vanessa, the already small room seemed to draw in even closer.

Torres was also showing the strain from the night's events but diffcrently. She remained polished outwardly, her hair still fixed and her makeup in place, but the telltale signs of Dianna's nerves didn't elude Vanessa. The jittery hand motions and bouncing knee exposed the true extent of the detective's anxiety.

As for herself, Vanessa had seen her image in the mirror. The face looking back at her was unrecognizable, but then again, so was the whirl of events surrounding her. Mascara-laden tear tracks on her cheeks and the mostly-loose ponytail hanging down her back gave her the look of someone who had just escaped a tornado. But what shook her most about her appearance was the deep sadness in her eyes. Her spirit was darker than she could remember at any time in her life.

Shifting uncomfortably, Torres finally raised her eyes to look at Vanessa. "I'm so sorry, and this sucks, but I know you understand."

"Of course. Let's get it over with."

"Okay. Start with yesterday morning, and go through your entire day."

Vanessa steeled herself and began. "I got up around seven, mainly because Kasen got me up. I made sure he had breakfast, a bath, and then got him dressed. We got in the car, and I dropped him off at pre-school."

"What school is that?"

"Southlake Enrichment."

Torres made a note. "And what time was that?"

"8:30 or so."

"Okay. Go ahead."

"I went back home, did some chores around the house, then called Rob."

"What was the nature of that call?"

"I was just checking in." Vanessa's eyes shifted to the floor. "We've been having some issues. He'd started sleeping at the shop recently."

"And was he okay? Did he sound normal?"

"Yes. We didn't talk long, but I told him I would call later."

Torres bobbed her head. "And what time was the call?"

"I don't have my phone, but I would guess just before lunch."

Torres paused, looking up at her. "Where's your phone?"

"I left it at the shop. That's why I returned and found…"

Torres nodded. "That's right, I remember now. Continue."

Vanessa sucked in enough air to restart her account. "I went back to the pre-school and picked up Kasen. We went over to my sister's for lunch, and afterward, I left him there."

SHADOW OF DOUBT

"What time was that?"

"Probably 1:00. Anyway, from there, I went to my lawyer's office."

"This is the one representing you in the appeal of your suspension?"

"Yes. His name is Conrad Donner, and I was in his office until 3:30. From there, I went to the firing range."

Torres froze. "The firing range?"

She nodded. "It helps me. I can focus on shooting rather than on other things."

"Other things?"

"Yeah, like the ones not going well."

"What range did you use?"

"The department's. I'm on suspension, not exiled."

"Were these the clothes you wore to the range?"

Vanessa looked down at her jeans and blue, V-neck top. "Yeah, but why…oh, gunshot residue. I'm sure you'll find some."

Torres forced a weak smile. "We need to do a test anyway."

"Of course, but you don't really think I killed Rob, do you?"

Torres avoided Vanessa's stare. "Vanessa, I'm just doing my job. I'll get the GSR test."

****

Lieutenant Savage stood next to Captain Morris in the darkened observation room, watching Vanessa while Morris watched the video recording of the session. The wall clock showed 8:15. Savage already felt as if he'd been up for days.

Vanessa's video was being evaluated by the captain as it was happening and would be watched, studied, and reviewed further many times by a large number of people. A long line of individuals, from the chief to the district attorney and beyond, would be asked for their opinion. This held true for the 911-call as well, and Savage was uneasy with how detached Vanessa's voice had sounded on that recording.

Nothing brought more intense scrutiny than an officer-related death. Every question asked and every answer given would be examined over and over. The goals included making sure there were no holes in stories, the detectives missed nothing, and that Vanessa was treated fairly. In other words, they had to make certain the job was done right.

After seeing the crime scene for himself, Savage was impressed with the professional strength Vanessa was showing in an unimaginably difficult situation. Just as important, she also seemed to be reflecting the appropriate level of shock—whatever that was—for a wife who had just lost her husband.

It always troubled him when someone pointed at a suspect and said, "They're not acting right." As if there was a standard written down in some book. Still, those who watched the interview video later would weigh her reactions and emotions to each question, just as he was doing now.

Like him, they'd watch for the signs of a lie, a hint of evasiveness, or the miniscule reflections of an untruth. And like him, those inside the fraternity of officers would pray they didn't see any of those things.

Neither he nor Morris had spoken since the interview started. Despite that, the atmosphere said one thing. *This is bad!*

Torres returned to the interview room with the gunpowder test kit and proceeded to swab Vanessa's hands, arms, and clothing. While Torres secured the samples, Vanessa crossed her arms and slumped farther into her chair.

Torres restarted the interview. "What time did you leave the range, and where did you go?"

Vanessa sighed. "Around six. I called Rachel and asked her to keep Kasen overnight."

"Why?"

"Because I was hoping to see Rob."

"At the shop?"

"No, not at the shop…at home."

"And did you?"

Vanessa shook her head. "I got home around six-thirty and tried calling him but got no answer. I waited until 11:00, but he didn't show."

"Were you home alone all evening?"

"Yes."

"Did you speak to anyone?"

"My sister and Kasen. I called around 8:30 to tell him goodnight."

Torres paused long enough to flip the page on her notebook. "Okay, you said you waited until 11:00. What did you do then?"

"I tried calling Rob again."

"At the shop?"

Vanessa nodded. "And?"

"And this time, he answered."

Torres was asking questions without looking up. From his vantage point, it was easy for Savage to see why. It seemed nobody wanted the interview over more than Dianna did.

The door to the observation room opened, allowing a flash of light inside, before being closed again. When his eyes adjusted, Savage realized Jason had joined them.

Jason's gaze traveled immediately to the scene on the other side of the glass. "How's she doing?"

Savage shrugged. "So far, she appears to be holding up well. What's the status at the scene?"

"Doc Josie and her techs will be cataloguing the inside of the garage for most of the day."

"Find anything yet?"

Jason nodded. "A few things. Empty bank bag, broken cellphone, and an empty shell casing."

Sarah, her attention still fixed on the monitor, looked up. "Shell casing? What cal?"

"9 millimeter."

"Do you know what Layne carries?"

Jason sighed. "A 9 millimeter."

Sarah squeezed her eyes shut. "Great!"

Savage moved to the door. "Excuse me. I'll be right back."

He went out into the hall and over to the interview room door, tapping on it twice. Torres came outside. "Yes, sir?"

"Ask about the cellphone, a broken one was found, and if Rob kept money at the garage."

"Okay."

"And when you're done with the interview, secure her gun before she leaves."

Dianna's eyes widened slightly. "Very well."

She went back inside while he returned to the observation room and opened the door. "Jason."

Jason answered, his eyes never leaving the scene through the window. "Yes?"

"Out here."

Jason turned, his eyebrows arched. "Sir?"

"I need you out here."

"Okay…" Jason crossed the room and came out into the hallway. "Something wrong?"

"Too much for me to recount. I need you to go over to the home of Detective Layne's sister. We need a statement from her before Vanessa leaves here."

"What sort of statement?"

"Timeline. We need her version of phone calls, pick-up and drop-off of the boy, everything. We'll need to compare it against Vanessa's story."

"Forgive me, sir, but it sounds like you're treating Vanessa as the primary suspect rather than a witness."

He stared at his detective for several moments, weighing his next words. Jason would accuse him of jumping to conclusions, but the truth was, people were almost always murdered by someone they knew. Still, he didn't want to be guilty of doing that very thing.

"We just need to make sure everything possible is done that makes this investigation above reproach. I think getting a statement from Vanessa's sister is prudent."

Jason hesitated briefly then nodded. "Of course. I'll take care of it now."

"Good. Let me know when you're back."

Savage returned to the observation room to find the questioning—and his boss's intensity—had both amped up. Torres flipped the page on her notebook again.

"You mentioned your cellphone. It was found at the scene with the screen broken. Do you know how that happened?"

Just a brief hesitation, then a sigh. "I did it."

"You did what?"

"I broke the phone."

"How?"

"I threw it."

Torres stopped and looked up, irritation showing on her face. Vanessa was suddenly making her pull teeth. "Why did you throw it?"

Another hesitation. "Something Rob said made me angry."

"So you threw it at Rob?"

A nod. "It was just a momentary lapse."

Torres was staring directly at Vanessa now. "What did he say?"

This time, the hesitation was much longer, and Vanessa's gaze moved to the floor. "He said there was someone…"

Her voice trailed off, and Torres had to push for the answer.

"I'm sorry, Vanessa, can you say that again?"

Vanessa looked up, tears returning to her eyes. "He said there was someone else."

It was Dianna's turn to hesitate. "I see…was there more?"

"That our marriage was over."

Torres pushed a box of tissues over to Vanessa. "Would you like another cup of coffee?"

Vanessa shook her head. "No. I want to finish." She used tissues to dry her eyes and face then looked up. "I'm ready."

Torres nodded and looked back at her notes, obviously struggling to refocus. "Uh… Okay… So, what happened after you threw the phone?"

"I left."

"And what time was that, do you know?"

"11:30, maybe. I'm not certain."

"When did you return to the garage to get your phone?"

Vanessa shifted nervously in her seat, causing both Savage and Morris to focus intently on her face. This was the critical moment. She had returned either to shoot him or to find him already down. It couldn't be both. The timeline would eventually reveal which.

Vanessa appeared to steel herself. "It was right before 12:30. I pulled up and saw the door was open. As I approached, I could see…I could see a…I could see Rob on the floor."

"What did you do?"

"I checked to see if anyone was still there then felt for a pulse."

"Did you find one?"

She shook her head. "He was gone. I tried to gather myself then called 9-1-1."

Torres made a few more notes. "Just a couple more questions, Vanessa. Did your husband keep money at the shop?"

"Sometimes. Mostly if he didn't have time to get to the bank."

"Where did he keep it?"

"A bank bag in the filing cabinet."

"Okay. Thanks."

Vanessa used the small table to push herself upright. "We're done?"

"Yes."

Vanessa moved toward the door. "Good. I need to go see my son."

"Of course." Torres had also stood. "One last thing."

"What?"

"I'll need your weapon."

Vanessa and Torres stared at each other, the distance between them close and charged.

Vanessa grimaced. "Why?"

"Just protocol. We want to run testing on it."

Vanessa looked toward the glass, prompting Savage to move toward the door. As if reading his mind, the captain held out her arm to block him. "Wait."

He hesitated.

Vanessa turned back to Torres, unsnapped her gun, and set it on the table. "Whatever you need."

After Vanessa left the room, Torres looked at the glass. "That was fun."

Morris keyed the mic button. "Nice job, Dianna."

SHADOW OF DOUBT

Chapter 4

Jason parked outside the home of Vanessa's sister, Rachel Underwood. She lived in an area known as the Far West Side, located between the Interstate 410 loop around downtown, and the 1604 loop that circled the outer part of the city. Alone with her two girls after her husband passed away, Rachel had finally given in to Vanessa's constant recommendation that Rachel move to San Antonio. A military pension provided support for her and the girls, including a modest, ranch-style home that was neat and orderly.

He'd called ahead, and the door opened quickly after he rang the bell. Rachel asked him in and led the way back to the kitchen.

"Coffee?"

He nodded. "Please. The girls in school?"

"Yes. They get home around three."

Rachel was no twin of Vanessa. Several inches shorter, with blonde hair and at least thirty pounds heavier than her detective sister, Rachel nonetheless was attractive in a matronly way.

Through the kitchen window, he spotted Kasen running around in the back yard, and Jason was struck by how closely the boy resembled his father, even at his young age.

Rachel set a cup of coffee in front of him. "How's Vanessa?"

"Holding up. As you know, she's pretty strong."

"Oh, I know. I wouldn't have survived my husband's death without her. Will she be home soon?"

"I'm not sure. They were still getting a full statement when I left the station."

She looked out the window at the young boy playing in the heat. "I haven't told him, but he's like his mother—perceptive. He can tell something is wrong."

Kasen kicked a soccer ball toward the house, striking the sliding glass door. When he looked up, both people were watching him. "Sorry, Aunt Rachel."

She waved at him and smiled.

Jason pulled out his notepad. "I don't want to take up any more of your time than necessary. I just need to ask a few brief questions."

"Of course."

"Tell me about yesterday, specifically your interactions with Vanessa and Rob."

She sighed. "Well, I haven't had much contact with Rob since things got tough between him and Vanessa. He used to drop Kasen off when Vanessa was busy, but since she's been suspended, I haven't seen him once."

"Okay. What about Vanessa yesterday?"

"She dropped Kasen off around 12:30, like she always does if she has something to do. Then, around six, she called and asked if I could keep him over night."

"Did she say why?"

Rachel nodded. "She was hoping she and Rob could talk about things."

"Did she say how? I mean, like over dinner or a date, say?"

"No, just that she would pick up Kasen for pre-school in the morning."

"Did you have any other contact with her last night?"

"Yes. She called around 8:30 to say goodnight to Kasen."

Jason put away his notepad. "Thank you; that's all I need."

"I'm glad to help. Jason?"

SHADOW OF DOUBT

"Ma'am?"

"Is Vanessa a suspect in Rob's death?"

"Not at this time. Why do you ask?"

Another smile, stronger this time. "Oh, you know. I watch all those cop shows, and they always suspect the spouse."

He laughed. "They do, don't they?"

"Yeah, but Vanessa could never do such a thing."

"That's certainly my sentiment. Goodbye, Rachel."

"Goodbye, Jason."

****

After his visit with Rachel, Jason had gone back to the station with one purpose—to watch the interview video. He needed to see her complete statement for himself. By the third time through, he was certain she was innocent. Torres, on the other hand, thought Vanessa was guilty.

When he finally arrived home that night, Sandy already had the kids in bed, and his dinner was waiting, albeit cold. While he changed and kissed the kids, their big dog Penny followed him around the house, seeming to sense his inner turmoil.

Back in the kitchen, Sandy had microwaved his dinner, and a bowl of steaming clam chowder was waiting for him. Sandy, her blonde hair pinned up, smiled.

"Do you want some crackers?"

"No, thanks. This is great."

She sat down at the kitchen table with him. "Kids asleep?"

"Not yet."

Despite her effort to keep things light, her brown eyes betrayed the sadness and worry she was struggling with, both for him and Vanessa. As he lifted a spoonful of hot soup to his mouth, he slid his other hand over on top of hers.

He knew she had a hundred questions but would let them wait, and for that, he was grateful. Exhaustion had taken hold. Not as much physically, but mentally and emotionally.

When he finished his soup, they moved to the family room. She brought them each a glass of wine and sat with him on the couch. He leaned in to her, and she played with his hair, brushing it off his forehead.

He let out a small sigh. "I love you, Sandy Strong…"

****

SHADOW OF DOUBT

The next morning, he awoke with a start. The sun was just beginning to filter through the sliding glass doors, and the house was still quiet. Confused at first, he looked down at the blanket that covered him. He was on the couch.

Pushing himself upright and rubbing his eyes, he finally cleared his vision enough to see the clock on the satellite box read 6:15. Sandy would be getting up soon, so he forced himself into the kitchen and started the coffee. Within minutes, the sound of little feet on the stairs announced the end to his quiet morning.

"Daddy!"

Nina had come around the corner first. He scooped her up and kissed her forehead. "Good morning, sweet pea."

Something attached itself to his leg. "Hi, Dad."

Jason set his daughter down and lifted David. "Hey, buddy. How's my boy?"

"Good."

Sandy was last. She had on a robe and wore her hair up in a ponytail. He put his son down and gave her a kiss.

"I guess I fell asleep on the couch?"

She grinned at him. "Very good, Detective."

"I'm sorry."

"Don't be. Did you get some rest?"

He stretched his arms and twisted at the waist. "I seem to be ready to go."

"Good. I'll get breakfast for the kids while you get ready."

"Okay, thanks."

When he returned a half hour later, the kids were in front of the TV in the family room, Penny was in the back yard, and Sandy was sitting at the table. He joined her and sipped his coffee.

She ventured a question. "What happened?"

"Well, the basic story is Vanessa visited Rob at the shop late. When she left, she forgot her phone. When she went back to get it, she found the door open and Rob on the floor. He'd been shot and was already gone."

Though she didn't have a plate in front of her, she played absently with a fork. "Poor Vanessa. It can't get any worse than that."

"She was holding it together pretty well, but I know her. There's a meltdown ahead, after the interviews and other stuff. I want to make sure she knows we're here for her."

"Absolutely. I'll call her this morning. What about the investigation?"

He tilted his head to one side, meeting her gaze. "I'm not sure. They had each of us doing different things. Hopefully, I can get up to speed when I arrive at the precinct."

"Will you let me know what you find out?"

"If I'm not swamped."

She nodded and kissed his forehead. "Fair enough."

He suddenly remembered the newspaper. "I'll be right back."

Out on the driveway lay the orange bag containing the San Antonio News. The heat of the day was already pressing in on the city as he retrieved it. He scooped it up and retreated into the air conditioning before unrolling it.

SAN ANTONIO MAN GUNNED DOWN IN HIS BUSINESS
Victim was husband of San Antonio P.D. Detective

(Devin James, Major Crimes Reporter)

Robert Layne, owner of Layne Body Shop, was gunned down inside his business early yesterday morning. The body shop is located in the 800 block of Broadway and is just one of several businesses in the area.

The victim was found by his spouse, Vanessa Layne. She is a homicide detective with the San Antonio police department.

When asked if she was a suspect, the supervising investigator declined to comment.

District Attorney Danny Lusk, when asked if the victim's wife would be fully investigated, issued a statement that read, in part: "We do not take into account a person's standing, within the community or otherwise, when making a decision on whether to prosecute or not."

"That no-class jerk!"

Sandy had come around the corner. "Who?"

"James. He can't resist sticking it to Vanessa or the department."

"What did he say?"

Jason handed her the paper. "Read for yourself. I've got to finish getting ready."

She took the paper and read it while following him to the bedroom. "Who is the 'supervising investigator' he refers to?"

"Good question. He asked me for info, but I refused to answer. I guess it could be me, even though I wasn't supervising anything."

"So who is?"

"Take your pick of the big dogs. Morris, Savage, or even Murray, for all I know."

SHADOW OF DOUBT

She read a little farther while he finished getting dressed. Finally, she threw the paper in the trashcan. "He does his best to make her look like the obvious killer."

"That sounds like Devin."

"What's he got against Vanessa?"

"I don't know. It goes back to the days before I made detective."

He headed for the den, kissed the kids then Sandy. "I'll see you tonight for dinner."

She smiled. "Hope so. Love you."

He climbed into his car and headed for the precinct, ignoring the fact he was driving a little too fast.

****

When the elevator doors opened on the third floor of the precinct, Jason found Torres waiting to take a ride back down. "Jason, perfect timing."

"Thanks. For what?"

"Savage wants us to take Vanessa back out to the garage. I was going to call you to meet me there."

"Is Vanessa also meeting us there?" He was unable to conceal his irritation.

"No. I was on my way to pick her up."

"I'll get her."

Torres hesitated then looked over her shoulder toward the lieutenant's office. The door was closed. "Uh, okay. Why don't we go together?"

"That's fine. I'll drive."

"Sure… Okay."

Jason had never stepped off the elevator, instead holding the door open during their conversation. Torres now joined him.

Riding in silence, Jason tried to interpret his surliness. Torres hadn't done anything to him or said anything wrong. Nothing had been conveyed to suggest Vanessa was the shooter, other than by Devin James, and it was clear Savage was trying to protect the department against a biased investigation.

Nevertheless, *something* was bothering him—something that went beyond worry for his partner or the loss of his friend. Maybe his imagination was playing tricks on him, but since the discovery of the victim's identity, it seemed as if he was being pushed to the outside of the investigation.

Get the cars towed; interview the sister; meet at the garage.

All peripheral tasks to the main investigation. At the same time, Torres had interviewed Vanessa and briefed the lieutenant. In the back of his mind though, he knew the truth. He was lucky to have any role in the investigation considering his relationship with Vanessa and Rob.

The elevator doors slid open, and Torres stepped off. "I called Vanessa about thirty minutes ago. She's expecting us."

"Good."

"The report from Doc Josie on the interior of the garage should be ready this afternoon. We can compare it to what Vanessa finds."

"Makes sense. As of right now, we don't have a motive for the killing, so maybe she can help with that."

"Yeah. Maybe."

They got into Jason's car and drove in silence to Vanessa's. When they pulled up, Vanessa was watching for them and came outside immediately. He watched her walk toward the car.

If she'd slept at all the night before, he couldn't tell. Her hair was down and appeared to be hastily brushed. A t-shirt and jean shorts helped her deal with the heat, but both hung on her.

She climbed into the back seat on his side, and he looked up in the rearview to get a sense of her mood. What he saw was darkness and agony.

"Hey, Vanessa."

"Hey."

Jason pulled out of the driveway and headed toward the shop. "You get any sleep last night?"

"Not much."

"How's Kasen?"

She was staring blankly out the window. "He doesn't understand, of course. I tried to explain Daddy wouldn't be home anymore, and that made him cry, but death is not a concept easily grasped by a four year old."

Torres had turned in her seat to look at Vanessa. "It's a hard concept for an adult to deal with. I can't imagine the impact on a child."

"He's staying with my sister for a few days."

Torres tried a smile. "Kids are resilient. They can handle some stuff better than us grown-ups."

Vanessa nodded absently. "I hope you're right."

While they drove in silence, Jason continued to check on his long-time partner, lifting his eyes to the rear-view mirror every minute or so. She remained distracted, even disconnected, until they pulled up in front of Layne Body Shop. Then she began to shake.

Jason got out and opened Vanessa's door. "You okay?"

SHADOW OF DOUBT

Vanessa's gaze fixed on Torres, who was unlocking the shop door. "I really don't want to go back in there."

Jason crouched down so he was face to face with her. "Hey, look at me."

She shifted her stare to meet his. He was unnerved by the lifeless veil that covered her normally bright-blue eyes. It appeared almost as if she'd checked out permanently.

"Vanessa, you can do this. He's not in there, and it's just a garage. You're not searching for evidence. All we need to know is if something is missing. Okay?"

She stared into his eyes for several moments then signaled her agreement by reaching for the door handle. "Let's get this over with."

"My feeling, exactly. Just wander through the shop, and check what you see against your memory."

She nodded, and they made their way through the open door. Torres was already in the office, searching through the desk drawers again.

Vanessa paused by the entrance, and despite the determined effort reflected on her face, Jason watched her focus move to the bloodstain where Rob's body had been. He flipped on the overhead lights and did his best to distract her.

"Start here on the right and move around the shop in a circle, okay?"

"Okay."

He followed in her footsteps as she walked around the space. She would intermittently pause then move on. She made it all the way around and back to the door without indicating she'd noticed anything.

She looked at Jason. "I don't know much about his tools, but the compressor is still here. It was one of the most expensive things in here. That and some diagnostic equipment."

"Do you see it?"

"Yes. The red boxes over there."

"Okay. Let's look in the office."

They joined Torres in the small space and waited while Vanessa looked around.

"His cellphone? Did you find his phone?"

Jason shook his head. "No. Where would he keep it?"

"On the desk. He would turn it off most of the time and just take calls on the shop phone, but it should be laying on his desk."

"Can you describe it?"

"It's an iPhone. The number is 555-4971."

Torres had her pad out and made a note.

Vanessa pointed at the desk's center drawer. "Was his gun in there?"

Jason looked at Torres, whose eyes widened noticeably. Torres shook her head, and Jason opened the drawer.

"There was no gun found, Vanessa. Would he always keep it in this drawer?"

Vanessa nodded. "As far as I knew."

"What was the gun, and when did he get it?"

"It was a Browning 9 millimeter. I bought it for him as a birthday gift two years ago. I wanted him to have something here in the shop to protect himself."

Torres was writing more notes. "Did he know how to use it?"

"Yes. We went to the range together several times."

The caliber wasn't lost on Jason.

Could Rob have been killed by his own gun? Or did the killer steal the gun?

Jason turned Vanessa's attention toward the file cabinet.

"We found an empty bank bag in the top drawer. Is there any way to tell if he had money in the shop on the night he was killed?"

Vanessa shrugged. "You could check his deposit records. If he hadn't made one in a day or two, he likely had money here."

Torres added the information to her notes. "Is there anything else missing that you can see?"

Vanessa, who appeared to be getting more exhausted with each passing minute, shook her head wearily. "That's all that comes to mind. I'm sorry."

Torres nodded at Jason to indicate she was done.

Jason smiled at Vanessa. "You did great. Come on, we'll take you home."

SHADOW OF DOUBT

John C. Dalglish

Chapter 5

Jason had offered to buy lunch for Vanessa at Stumpy's Bar-B-Q, their favorite restaurant near the precinct, but she had begged off.

"I just want to go home, if that's okay."

"Of course."

After dropping her off, Torres suggested they go anyway. "It's pushing noon, and I'm hungry. You?"

"I guess."

The place was busy, as usual, but they had come in early enough that they had no trouble finding a table. Dianna ordered a giant plate of pulled pork nachos, but Jason settled for a sandwich, and even it wasn't disappearing from his plate with any urgency.

"Detective Strong, how are you doing?"

SHADOW OF DOUBT

Caught off guard, Jason looked up to see the face of Devin James. "I'm eating, Devin. Another time, please."

"Of course. Detective Torres, do you have a moment?"

Despite the hostile stare Jason threw her way, Dianna answered. "What for?"

"I was wondering if you had identified a suspect in the shooting of Rob Layne."

"No comment."

"So the report that Vanessa Layne is being looked at as such could be true."

Jason kicked back his chair and moved between Torres and the reporter.

"Look, James! Your editor may let you get away with innuendo and speculation, but you won't find any help for it here. Now I'm going to ask you once more. Leave us alone to eat our lunch in peace."

The reporter briefly met Jason's glare then backed away. He leaned around Jason and smiled at Torres. "Nice seeing you again, Detective. Good day, Jason."

Waiting until the reporter had left the restaurant before sitting back down, Jason avoided Dianna's gaze.

When she finished her nachos, she pushed her plate aside and studied him. "What was that all about?"

"What?"

"Oh. Come on. You two obviously have a history."

Jason pushed his plate away, half the sandwich still on it. "We have had some dealings in the past, most of which were civil."

"Well, that conversation was not one of them."

"No, but less because of me than because of Vanessa."

She leaned back in her seat, curiosity mixed with confusion painted on her face. "Care to explain?"

"I'm not sure I can. Vanessa made detective before I did, and something occurred between her and James that was not good. I never found out what it was, but he seems to have it out for her, even after all this time."

"Vanessa never told you about it?"

"I never asked."

"I see."

Jason's phone buzzed in his pocket. He pulled it out and checked a text message. "Lieutenant says we have a couple reports on our desks."

"Okay then. I'm ready if you are."

"Let's go."

****

SHADOW OF DOUBT

Back at the precinct, Jason dropped into his chair at the same time Torres occupied Vanessa's desk. They were facing each other as both picked up a report and started reading. Jason finished first.

"The gunshot residue test was positive. Vanessa had it on her sleeve and arm, but she'd been to the range earlier in the day."

"That's right."

"So this is not much help. What have you got?"

"The canvas reports done by officers at the local businesses."

"Anything?"

She looked up at him, and he sensed she was about to tell him something he didn't want to hear.

"A man by the name of Renaldo Garza owns a t-shirt screen-printing business across from the body shop. He said he was finishing up an order due the next day when he saw a yellow car speed away from the garage around midnight."

"Did he hear gunshots?"

Torres shook her head. "He had earbuds in and was listening to the radio."

"That matches Vanessa's statement of what happened after she threw her phone at Rob."

Torres nodded. "Yes, but the time is wrong. Vanessa claimed she left the shop around 11:30 then returned about an hour later."

"So the guy has the time wrong."

"He claims to be certain because he was listening to a baseball game."

Jason and Torres stared at each other, as Jason worked to digest the information. The timeline of any murder was critical in solving most cases, and something that doesn't fit is a red flag to any detective.

Torres turned back to the remainder of the interviews. After several minutes, she threw the stack of papers onto the desk. "That's the only person who claimed to see anything."

Lieutenant Savage got off the elevator and stopped by their desks. "How are we coming along?"

Torres looked at Jason then at their boss. "Slow. Nothing significant yet."

"Keep at it. Is there anything you need?"

"Actually, yes. Can you subpoena the phone records of both Rob and Vanessa Layne?"

"Put the numbers on my desk, and I'll take care of it."

Jason's desk phone rang. "Homicide. Detective Strong."

"Jason, it's Doc Davis."

"Hey, Doc. Have you got something for us?"

"Can you come down here?"

"Of course. On our way."

Jason hung up. "Doc Davis wants to see us."

Torres lunged to her feet. "Man, I hope he's got something."

Savage stepped aside. "Don't let me get in your way."

Jason joined her on the way to the elevator, but she took the stairs, instead. Reluctantly, he followed. When they reached the basement, as he'd suspected, Jason had to pause and suck in a little extra air. More winded than he cared to admit, Torres on the other hand was already at the door to the morgue. He dragged himself after her.

Inside the sterile room, illuminated with an excessive number of overhead lights, they found Doc Davis standing next to an autopsy table. When he spotted them, he waved them around to his side.

"You're going to want to see this."

Surprised by Doc's lack of small talk, Jason quickly picked up the tension within the big coroner's jaw muscles. Whatever he was about to tell them, Doc wasn't looking forward to saying it.

Jason and Torres leaned over Rob Layne's body to look at the area Doc pointed out to them. They were looking at the entrance wound on Rob's chest. Doc pulled a pen out of his pocket and made a circle motion above the wound, without touching it.

"The size of the entry wound suggests a large-caliber weapon."

Jason nodded, stepping back slightly from his friend. "That's what you thought at the scene."

"I know. Now come with me."

Doc walked across the room, and Jason and Torres followed. Doc reached for the switch on the x-ray viewing board and turned on the backlight. Illuminating two different angles of a torso, Doc used the same pen to point out a pair of bright spots on the scans.

"You see these two bright spots?"

Both Jason and Torres nodded.

"Do you know what they are?"

Jason had seen them a thousand times. "Slugs?"

"Exactly. Two of them."

Torres stared at the coroner with a vacant look. "And?"

Jason was already a step ahead. "Rob was shot twice?"

Doc nodded. "I'm afraid so."

Jason squeezed his eyes shut. "Crap!"

Torres stared at Jason then turned to Doc. "What am I missing?"

Sucking in a deep breath, then exhaling loudly, he clued her in. "Two shots with such tight targeting suggests…"

The bulb finally went on for Dianna. "A very good marksman…or woman."

Jason nodded. "Did you retrieve the slugs, Doc?"

"Yeah, and one won't be much good because it struck a rib on the way in. The other still had markings, and I sent it to Doc Josie."

"Good. Anything else from the examination?"

"Just confirming the caliber."

"9 millimeter?"

"Yes."

Jason headed out of the morgue, followed by Torres, and crossed to the forensic lab. The interior was much the same as the morgue, with abundant light fixtures above stainless steel tables, minus the blood and body parts.

Doc Josie was sitting at her desk, and the warm greeting Jason usually received was absent here, too. He tapped on the doorframe, and she looked up through tired eyes.

"Hi, Jason, Dianna. My report on ballistics is done but not the processing of the cars."

Jason shrugged. "We'll take what we can get."

"Okay. Well, first off and most importantly, the slugs did not match the test slugs from Vanessa's gun, nor did the firing pin marks on the casing. Her weapon was not the one that fired the fatal shots."

Jason smiled. "That's excellent."

Josie nodded. "I thought so, too. I found a cellphone inside Rob Layne's car, but it had a dead battery. Otherwise, we've found nothing else up to now. I still need to spray luminol in the interior for traces of blood, but I didn't find any obvious smears in either car."

Torres had her notepad out. "What about the garage itself?"

Josie sighed. "A boatload of fingerprints. It will take time to process them all, but we did process the partials we lifted from the shop phone. They weren't usable because of foreign matter."

"What was on the phone?"

"Mostly paint."

Jason turned to go. "You'll send us the report when it's ready?"

"Of course."

"Thanks. We'll get out of your hair."

SHADOW OF DOUBT

Josie was already back at work when they headed for the door.

****

Lieutenant Savage spotted them as soon as they stepped off the elevator and met them at their desks.

"I need both of you in my office ten minutes from now. Bring your files, so we can go over what you have."

Jason exchanged looks with Torres. "What we have?"

"I want an idea where this case is heading. We'll whiteboard it, and then discuss the next step."

"But we're nowhere near figuring it out."

Savage turned to Torres. "Can we clear Detective Layne?"

Torres hesitated, shifting from one foot to the other like a teenager at the front of the class. "No, sir."

Jason's jaw tightened. "But there's little to suggest she did it, either."

"I want both sides." Savage headed back to his office. "Ten minutes!"

Torres dropped into her chair, avoiding Jason's stare, and pulled out her notepad. He was still standing, glaring down at her, measuring his words.

"Do you still believe Vanessa shot her husband?"

Keeping her eyes focused on the notes in front of her, she shrugged. Jason sensed his blood pressure hitting new heights.

"I've known her for years, and I'm telling you, she could never do it."

Torres sighed and leaned back in her chair, finally locking eyes with him. "That's the point, isn't it?"

Jason's brow furrowed. "What do you mean?"

"You've known Vanessa forever, whereas, I have not. While I like her, our job is to follow where the evidence leads, not where we want it to go."

"Are you suggesting I would look the other way if Vanessa was guilty?"

"No! I'm not suggesting anything, but have you asked yourself if you are remaining neutral and unbiased in your examination of the case?"

Jason glared down at her. "Perhaps I should ask you the same question."

"Seriously! What motive would I have to pin this crime on Vanessa?"

He stood there, his breathing rapid and his face flushed. What answer wouldn't seem ridiculous?

SHADOW OF DOUBT

Jealousy, desire for promotion, favoritism with Savage, public accolades for exposing a guilty detective.

None made any sense, and even with his anger, he couldn't bring himself to say them out loud. He finally dropped into his chair, his agitation flowing from him like blood from a wound. Torres was still watching him, apparently waiting for an answer.

"I'm sorry, Dianna. I was out of line."

She leaned forward, her voice dropping to a whisper, her eyes fixed on his.

"Look, I get it. She's been your partner and your friend for a long time. None of us wants to think someone we care about could do something like commit murder, and I'm not saying she did, but it wouldn't be the first time someone made a mistake. You and I both know that none of us are immune to the pain and emotion that can drive us to do crazy things."

"It's more than that, Dianna. It goes against everything she is."

"I believe you. Look, let's just give the lieutenant the timeline, let him ask his questions, then we'll take a fresh look afterward."

He nodded. "Fair enough."

****

A few minutes later, they'd entered the lieutenant's office to find him on the phone. Torres had gone to the whiteboard hanging at the far end of the office and started making notes.

    8:30 a.m.—drops Kasen at school.
    11:30—Called and spoke with victim.
    Noon—Picked up son
    12:30 p.m.—Leave son with sister.
    1:00—Appointment with lawyer
    3:30—Leave lawyer's office
    4:30—Target practice at gun range.
    6:00—Called sister and asked her to keep son overnight.
    6:30—Arrived home and called victim-No answer.
    8:30—Calls sister to say goodnight to Kasen.
    11:00—Called and spoke with victim.
    11:15—Arrives at shop and has argument.
    11:30—Leaves garage
    12:30—Calls 911

By the time she was done, both the lieutenant and Jason were watching her. Savage leaned back in his chair, running his hand over his scalp. "This is the timeline given by Vanessa for her activities, correct?"

"Yes, sir."

"Okay. Verifications?"

Torres consulted her notes. "Some."

"Such as?"

Jason had his pad out. "The sister verifies Vanessa dropped her son off at 12:30 and called her at 6:00. She also verified the purpose of the call and that Kasen spent the night."

"Kasen? Son?"

"Yes, sir."

"What else?"

Dianna looked up. "I spoke with the school, and they verified both the dropping off and picking up of Kasen at the times Vanessa gave."

"Lawyer?"

She looked back at her notes. "The lawyer's secretary verified the appointment and that it lasted until approximately 3:30."

Savage had reverted to his habit of short, direct questions. "Gun range."

"Again, checks out. In fact, she was a regular, showing up as often as three times a week."

"Phone calls?"

Jason shrugged. "We can verify only the 9-1-1. We're still waiting on phone records."

"Vanessa's gun?"

"Not a match.

"Anything not check out?"

Torres looked at Jason, who gestured for her to go ahead.

She turned back to the lieutenant. "So far, we have one issue."

"Which is?"

"A man working across the street that night said a yellow car sped away from the body shop around midnight. That puts her leaving very close to the time of death."

Savage stared at the timeline. "So...she may not have been gone when the shooting took place but in fact, left afterward."

The atmosphere in the room was suddenly thick with tension.

The lieutenant leaned forward, rubbing his head again. "And that is why we can't clear Detective Layne?"

"That and something else."

"Which is?"

Jason shifted in his chair. "We have yet to locate a missing 9 millimeter gun belonging to the victim."

"Suggesting what?"

"The missing gun may have been the murder weapon, and the shooter dumped it after the shooting."

"She tell you about the gun?"

"Yes."

"This just keeps getting worse! Okay, so we can't clear Layne yet. What about other suspects or motives? Anything?"

Jason nodded. "Robbery is possible, as is an irate customer, but we haven't had a chance to fully check those."

"Fair enough. What else?"

Torres came over and sat down. "We know Rob Layne was having an affair, but we haven't been able to get a name. We're hoping the phone records will solve that."

"Angry mistress? Jealous husband?"

Torres lifted her hands, palms up. "Could be. We just don't know."

"Okay. You two go back to work; I've got to call the captain."

John C. Dalglish

Chapter 6

Opting not to hang around the precinct and stare at each other while they hoped for the phone records to show up, Jason and Torres headed over to Vanessa's place. He wanted to check on her, and Torres had more questions… Two birds—one stone.

Vanessa answered the door in sweat pants and an SAPD t-shirt. She looked as if she may have just rolled out of bed. "Hey. I wasn't expecting visitors."

Jason grinned at her. "Clearly!"

She looked down at herself and laughed. "I guess you could tell. Come in."

The tidy home Jason had visited many times was now in disarray, not that he found it surprising. "Where's Kasen? Still with your sister?"

"Yeah. Rachel's been great."

"Get any sleep last night?"

"Not much. Sandy called me this morning."

"She's worried about you. We all are."

Torres, abnormally quiet to this point, nodded her agreement. Vanessa pointed toward the couch.

"You want to sit down. I was just going to make some coffee."

Jason shook his head. "Not for me. We just have a few questions."

Vanessa rubbed her eyes. "I figured. Let me start the coffee anyway, and I'll be right back."

Five minutes later, Vanessa returned, pushed some unfolded laundry off the loveseat, and sat down. "What did you need to know?"

Torres had her pad out. "Which bank did Rob use for the business? The money bag we found was from a defunct savings and loan."

"Yeah, they were bought out by Select Credit Union. Rob would make deposits at a branch on North Pine."

"Did your husband ever mention an angry client? Maybe someone who threatened him?"

Vanessa shook her head. "No. I've been racking my brain, trying to think of anyone who might have wanted to hurt Rob. I can't think of a single person."

Jason scooted forward on the couch, closing the distance between him and his friend. He lowered his voice, as if he might reveal something unpleasant to an unseen eavesdropper.

"Rob said he had been unfaithful…"

Anguish raced across Vanessa's face. "Yes."

"Did he tell you her name?"

Blinking tear-filled eyes, she shook her head.

Jason reached out and touched her hand. "I'm sorry. I had to ask."

She bobbed her head, wiping at her eyes. "I know."

Jason stood, and Torres followed suit. Vanessa remained seated, her head in her hands. They moved toward the door, but something stopped Jason.

"Vanessa?"

She looked up through moist eyes. "Yeah?"

"There was a photo missing from the wall in the office. Do you know what the picture might have been?"

She pointed at the hall table. "It's right there."

Jason turned and picked up the small frame. Vanessa and Rob were sitting in the yellow Challenger, Vanessa in the driver's seat. A giant red bow was stuck to the car's hood. Jason had never seen the photo before.

"This was on the wall in the shop?"

Vanessa nodded.

Jason looked at Torres. "I don't guess we need this, do you?"

"I can't imagine why we would."

Jason put the photo back. "Call me or Sandy if you need anything, okay?"

"I will...and thanks."

****

Jason and Torres pulled up in front of the yellow-brick structure emblazoned with the name *Ella Austin Community Center.* A black, wrought-iron fence surrounded a kids' playground equipped with oversized plastic slides and swings.

Torres double-checked the address. "This is it. Don't usually find a playground at a bank."

"Apparently, the credit union branch is inside."

They got out and climbed the concrete steps to the large, plate-glass door. Inside the lobby, the financial institution was to the left, the community center to the right.

They turned left and approached a desk. Jason showed his badge.

"We're with San Antonio P.D. Is the branch manager in?"

A non-descript woman in her mid-forties nodded, picked up the phone without speaking, and punched a couple numbers. A crossword puzzle on her desk seemed infinitely more interesting to her than interacting with Jason and Torres. "Marilyn, there're two detectives here to see you."

The conversation ended abruptly, and the crossword regained the receptionist's attention.

Coming from somewhere at the back of the room, a gray-haired woman in business attire was smiling as she hurried toward them. "How can I help you, Detectives?"

"We need some information on one of your clients," Jason showed her his badge, and unlike the receptionist, the manager studied it with interest.

"Oh? Well, follow me, and I'll see if I can help." She led them back in the direction from which she'd come. "Who's the client?"

"Rob Layne of Layne Body Shop."

They turned into a small office containing a desk and not much else. A couple photos on the wall, a citation for service to the credit union, and a mass-produced painting of a sailboat. The room reminded Jason of a cave but with less light.

She sat down and pointed at the two chairs opposite her. "Have a seat."

Torres accepted and pulled out her notepad. Jason opted for the fresh air of the hallway, and instead stayed leaning against the doorframe. Marilyn moved the computer mouse on her desk, and the monitor came to life.

"What information do you need about Mr. Layne?"

Jason shook his head. "Some basic data from his banking records."

Perplexed, the manager looked from Torres to Jason. "I'm not allowed to give out anything personal."

"Miss…"

"Kiffin—Marilyn Kiffin."

"Miss Kiffin, Rob Layne was killed last night."

"Oh my, that's terrible. What happened? A car accident?"

Jason shook his head slowly. "He was shot."

"Shot?" She appeared unable to process the news. "That doesn't seem possible. He was such a nice man."

"I'm afraid it's true."

"What information do you need?"

"We're interested in whether Mr. Layne made a deposit yesterday."

"I want to help, don't get me wrong, but I can't release his records without a warrant."

Torres folded her notepad and tucked it away, the lack of a need for it now apparent. "Look, we don't have to see his actual records, and at least for right now, we don't need a printout of them. Can you just tell us *if* he made a deposit yesterday?"

Marilyn stared at Torres for a few seconds then nodded once, as if she'd made up her mind. Tapping some numbers into the computer, she turned the monitor so only she could see it. Running her finger across the screen, she paused then looked up. "Yes, Mr. Layne made a deposit yesterday afternoon, just before three o'clock."

Torres stood. "Thank you."

Jason followed her as she made her way back to the lobby and came up to the crossword lady's desk. Torres leaned over the book and tapped one of the boxes. "A four letter word for *ill-mannered*—R-U-D-E."

She walked away, leaving the receptionist slack-jawed. Jason laughed as they reached the car.

"Nicely done. Reminds me of something Vanessa would do."

Torres smiled. "I'll take that as a compliment."

"It was meant as one."

SHADOW OF DOUBT

****

Forty-five minutes later, they'd arrived back at the precinct to find the phone records had still not arrived. Frustrated, Jason called and made sure the company was actually responding to the warrant. He was assured the records would be in first thing the next morning.

When he hung up, Torres was staring at him, her notepad open in front of her. "Nothing?"

"They promised us first thing tomorrow."

"Do you want to go over what we've got again?"

Jason sighed and dragged his hand across his chin. "Am I allowed to say no?"

"I would."

He laughed, despite his exhaustion. "What are you referring to?"

"Motives? We had five, but I think we're down to three."

"Which have we eliminated, in your mind?"

"In light of the deposit Rob made, I think robbery is unlikely. His phone wasn't taken, and none of the stuff considered valuable in the garage was stolen, either."

Jason nodded. "I agree, at least for now."

Torres flipped a page on her notes. "Vanessa said her husband had never mentioned an argument with a customer or anyone threatening him at his work, and everyone we talk to says he was a nice guy."

"We haven't worked our way through his customer log yet. We should probably run the names through our database. Maybe one of them had a record."

"Granted, that is something that needs to be done, but I think the irate customer is an unlikely motive."

He rubbed his chin again. "Okay. So that leaves us with angry mistress and jealous husband and…"

"Vanessa."

He stared at her. He wanted to tell her she was barking up the wrong tree, that it couldn't be Vanessa. But the truth was, with two motives down and only three left, the odds were less in Vanessa's favor than before.

Though he wanted to launch into another defense of his partner, he opted for diplomacy.

"I'm gonna call it a night. There's not much we can do until we have the phone records."

Torres, who appeared to have been holding her breath, sighed.

"Yeah. Me too."

Jason got up and headed for the elevator, followed by Dianna. This time, he took the stairs.

It's probably best to avoid an elevator ride where I might say something I regret.

****

When he arrived home, Sandy had dinner waiting. The kids had eaten already and were in the family room. The day weighed heavily on Jason, and ruffling the furry white neck of their big Pyrenees was good for his soul.

Sandy was being her usual understanding self, letting him unwind. He didn't envy the role she'd taken on. The only thing worse than seeing some of the things a detective sees, is being the wife of that detective.

As he pushed food around his plate, she broke the silence.

"Vanessa called a little while ago."

"Oh?"

"Yeah. The funeral has been scheduled for the day after tomorrow."

"Really? Doc Davis released the body?"

Apprehensiveness played across her face, and he immediately regretted his question. He reached over and laid his hand on hers. "I'm sorry. That's not something you should know."

"It's okay."

"Did she say where and when?"

"Yes. 9:30 at Colonial Funeral Home."

He raised an eyebrow. "Colonial? Isn't that where John Patton's service was?"

"It is. That's apparently one of the reasons she chose it."

"It's going to be a rough day for everyone concerned."

She kissed his forehead and smiled. "True, but at least you have me."

He raised her hand to his lips and kissed the back of her fingers. "And I'm a better man for it, too."

SHADOW OF DOUBT

John C. Dalglish

Chapter 7

Jason was first in the next morning, followed shortly by Torres. As usual, Lieutenant Savage was in before them both. Jason and Torres found the phone records waiting for them.

Jason lifted the two piles and held them up. "Your choice. Rob's business or Vanessa's cellphone?"

"Rob's business. No sign of the records on Rob's cellphone?"

"Nope. Must still be in the pipeline." He tossed one pile of records onto her desk. "There you go."

They were just getting ready to dig in when the door to the lieutenant's office opened. He came over and stopped by Jason's desk.

"You haven't forgotten about tomorrow, have you?"

He had. "Tomorrow?"

"The hearing."

SHADOW OF DOUBT

With everything going on, he had completely forgotten about the appeal hearing for his partner. As if Vanessa didn't have enough going on, she had to face the possibility of losing her job. "Oh, my…is that tomorrow?"

"9:00 a.m."

"Can't they put it off, considering the events of the last few days?"

"My understanding is that Vanessa wanted to go ahead with it. She's looking to put it behind her."

"Okay. I'll be there."

"Good. Once that's over, she can focus on her husband's funeral."

"You bet."

Savage then turned to Torres and handed her a post-it note. "This is something you need to look in to."

Torres accepted the offering. "What is it?"

"A phone message. Heather Franklin over at the SAPD's human resources department wanted to know if she could process the insurance paperwork on Rob Layne."

"What kind of paperwork?"

"That's what I asked her. Apparently, Vanessa and her husband had purchased an additional policy on him. Life insurance for one hundred thousand dollars."

Jason watched the news visibly impact Torres, who turned to stare at him with widened eyes. She let out a low whistle. "That's a lot of insurance."

He looked up at the lieutenant. "Do we have any details like when the policy was purchased?"

Savage pointed at the note. "Details would be why I gave you two the note. Perhaps you could follow up on it, being as you are crack investigators."

Jason managed a smile. "Yes, sir."

"Good. I'll be in my office."

Jason picked up his phone. Torres tipped her head in surprise. "Don't you want the number?"

"Nope. You call them and get the details. I'll call Vanessa and see what she has to say. Then we can compare notes."

Torres nodded and picked up her phone.

Vanessa answered quickly. "Hello?"

"Vanessa, it's Jason. How you doing this morning?"

"Fair. I managed a few hours of sleep last night."

"Good. Sandy told me the funeral had been scheduled. Is there going to be a graveside service?"

"No. Rob always said he wanted to be cremated."

The impending funeral seemed to choke the air out of him. "Oh...I didn't know."

The conversation stalled until Vanessa prodded him. "Jason?"

"Yeah?"

"Was there something else?"

"Oh...oh, yeah. Sorry. I lost my train of thought."

"That's fine. What is it?"

"It's about life insurance. Did you purchase an extra policy on Rob?"

"Yes...why?" An uneasiness had crept into her voice.

"When did you buy it?"

"Uh...I'm not sure. At least a year ago, I believe."

"Was Rob aware of the policy?"

"Of course."

"Why did you decide to buy it?"

Vanessa didn't hide her irritation. "Why do you normally buy insurance, Jason?"

He squeezed his eyes shut, chastising himself for being so blunt. "I'm sorry, Vanessa. I don't mean to sound so suspicious. We just learned about the policy, and I want to clear up any misunderstandings."

"I get it. Look, despite the fact I was getting rich as a detective..."

Jason grunted. "Yes?"

"Rob's income was the biggest part of what we had. He wanted me to be protected in the unlikely event… If something happened to him."

"Of course. I suspected as much."

"Listen, Jason, I need to go. Is there anything else?"

"Not right now. I'll talk to you later, okay?"

"Sure."

The phone clicked in his ear. Frustration welled up within him, both at his behavior with his friend and partner, as well as with the investigation as a whole. Vanessa couldn't be guilty of shooting Rob, but each time he thought he was getting close to clearing her, something else came up.

His gaze turned to the phone records on his desk. Thankful for a distraction, he started in on them while Torres finished her conversation with human resources. His primary interest was the day Rob was killed, and he quickly separated out the sheets from that twenty-four hour period.

He had just uncapped his yellow marker when Torres hung up. "Did you get a hold of Vanessa?"

"I did."

"So let's compare. When did she say she bought the policy?"

"At least a year ago."

Torres looked down at her pad. "Ten months, to be exact. Close enough. Did she say if Rob knew?"

"Yes, he did."

"Okay, well his signature was not on the policy. Only Vanessa signed it."

"Isn't that normal if she was buying the policy?"

Torres shrugged. "I guess, but it doesn't help us know if Rob was aware of what his life was worth to Vanessa."

Jason's face flushed. "Perhaps you should re-word that statement!"

She backpedaled. "I'm sorry. We still don't know for sure if Rob knew about the policy."

Jason nodded but held his tongue.

"Did Vanessa say why she bought the policy?"

"Yes. Apparently, Rob made the larger portion of their income through his body shop."

"Well, that fits with adding coverage on him. As a self-employed individual, he probably didn't have any coverage of his own."

An uneasy peace settled on them, Jason trying to calm down while Torres studied her notes further. When she didn't ask any more questions, he returned to the phone records. After highlighting each call and it's time on the day of the murder, he pulled up a typed copy of Vanessa's statement and began to compare the two.

The 11:30 a.m. call checked out, as did the phone call at 6:00 to Rachel. The 6:30 call also showed up as outgoing but not connected. That matched her statement that Rob did not answer her call about dinner. Also showing up was the call to say goodnight to Kasen.

After that, there was no activity until 11:05 p.m. when she retried Rob's number, this time getting an answer. The conversation lasted just four minutes. Again, this lined up with her statement. That was the last entry, which coincided with the phone being broken a half hour later. All of the calls had pinged off the tower near her home.

He sat back in his chair, both relieved and encouraged by the matching records. Torres was going over Rob's records with equal intensity. She had gotten to the last page when she looked up at Jason.

His adrenaline spiked. "What is it?"

An undertone of suspicion carried her words. "Didn't the 9-1-1 call register at 12:30 a.m. that morning?"

"I think so. Why?"

"That was the *second* call to 9-1-1. The first call was made at 12:18 a.m. and hung up the moment the operator answered."

"Are you sure?"

Torres slid the paper across the desk to where Jason could see it and laid her finger on the time stamp. "There it is."

"Did emergency dispatch call the number back?"

"I don't know. If they did, there was no answer."

Jason's good feelings about his search were quickly washed away by the implication of what Torres had found.

12:18 is much closer to the time of the shooting and puts Vanessa at the garage earlier than they previously believed. Did she take time to change the scene? Maybe she was making up her story. And why didn't she mention the call?

He pushed away the panic in his mind and tried to focus on real possibilities.

Torres was watching him. "What do you think, Jason?"

"I'm not sure. Perhaps she started to call but thought she heard the shooter."

"Maybe."

"Or is it possible Rob made a sound, and she stopped to check on him?"

Torres had become very deliberate, even cautionary in her tone.

"Also…possible."

"What do you think?"

She sucked in a deep breath. "I can tell you what I'm worried about."

"Okay, shoot."

"I'm worried she may have used the time to cover something up or get rid of the gun."

Jason didn't want to agree with her.

The lieutenant leaned out of his office. "You two."

They answered in unison. "Sir?"

"Press conference, one hour. You won't answer questions, but I want you there."

Savage disappeared back into his office.

Jason looked at Torres, and the dread on her face mirrored his own reaction to the news.

Torres said it for both of them.

"Greaaaat!"

****

The small room, a patrol briefing room turned press conference space, was surprisingly empty when Jason and Torres arrived with Lieutenant Savage. Usually, just about any murder investigation had a standard cast of characters who attended the press briefings, but only a handful were in the room today.

Front and center was Devin James, who nodded at Jason when he entered. Jason pretended not to notice. One TV station had sent a camera crew, and two smaller news organizations were represented, but that was it.

Standing behind the lieutenant, Jason nudged Torres. "Small crowd."

"Yeah. I wonder why."

Savage stepped to the podium and looked over the room. "Thanks for coming. I'm going to read a brief statement, and as the announcement said earlier, no questions will be taken at this time. The statement will be faxed to all news outlets."

Jason leaned closer to Torres. "That explains it. No questions allowed."

Savage cleared his throat and began to read.

"The San Antonio Police Department is currently investigating the death of Rob Layne. As reported elsewhere, he is the husband of Detective Vanessa Layne. At this time, no one has been charged with the murder or with anything related to Mr. Layne's death."

He flipped the page.

"Bexar County District Attorney Danny Lusk, as well as San Antonio Police Chief William Murray, want the public to be assured that this case will get the same scrutiny as all other homicides within our city. The truth will be sought out and the killer brought to justice. No favoritism, as alleged by some news sources, will be tolerated. All cases handled by this department will be thorough and fair, period."

He folded the sheets of paper and put them in his pocket. "Thank you."

The lieutenant had barely turned to leave when Devin jumped to his feet. His voice was louder than it needed to be in such a small room. "Is Vanessa Layne the prime suspect?"

Savage kept his eyes forward, his pace quickening toward the door.

"Is she being investigated at all?"

Jason and Dianna were close on the lieutenant's heels.

"Detective Strong, has Vanessa been cleared?"

Jason stopped and spun so quickly that the reporter took a step backward. "She is Detective Layne to you, James!"

SHADOW OF DOUBT

Before Devin could utter a response, Jason was out the door and on the elevator with Torres.

She was watching him closely. "Don't let him get under your skin, Jason."

"I don't get it. Why is he so intent on pinning Vanessa with this shooting?"

"Maybe he thinks the spouse is always responsible."

Jason shook his head in disagreement, as well as in an effort to clear his thoughts. "I don't know. James seems smarter than that."

The elevator doors opened on the third floor. Savage, who had apparently taken the stairs, was already at his desk. He was on the phone with someone, animated in his conversation. Jason guessed it was Captain Morris, who hadn't been at the news conference, which surprised Jason.

In fact, he'd expected she would have given the statement herself. Sarah Morris was the only one he'd ever seen who could put Devin James in his place. She could start and end a press conference with remarkable speed and efficiency, forcing even the most experienced reporter to wonder what happened.

As they walked to their desks, the lieutenant hung up and waved at them. "You two. Got a minute?"

They re-routed themselves to his office and went inside.

Savage stood and moved to the door. "Pull up a chair."

He closed the door while Jason and Torres did as instructed. When the lieutenant came back around his desk and sat down, Jason could sense the turmoil within the man. The series of events since the arrest in the Sam Bullock case, most involving Vanessa, were not what he'd hoped his new job would be focused on.

He dropped heavily into his chair. "I'm passing this on from Captain Morris, and it's not directed at any one person, understand?"

They nodded.

"From this moment forward, no information of any kind is to be revealed outside these walls. Nothing."

The lieutenant's gaze moved from Jason to Torres and back again, so Jason couldn't be sure if he was the target. Both he and Torres nodded again, neither opting to speak.

Intensity radiated from the big lieutenant. "Regardless of whether Vanessa is found to be culpable in the death of her husband, all facts will be gathered, and the district attorney will decide. We, myself included, are under strict orders to prevent any leaks."

Jason squirmed in his chair. Savage brought his eyes around to stare hard at him. "What is it, Jason?"

"Well…is a leak suspected?"

"My impression is yes, but it's only an impression. I was not privy to the conversations that resulted in this order. Both it and the statement I read to the press came from above me."

"Something must have happened to cause such concern."

Savage sighed. "All I know is someone, presumably in the press, was asking much too pointed questions about the investigation. The powers that be are worried that Detective Layne will be tried and convicted in the court of public opinion, and with her, the department."

It seemed obvious to Jason that Devin James had to be the one who'd prompted all this, but Jason had no way of knowing for sure.

Savage leaned back in his chair. "Are we clear on where we stand?"

Both Jason and Torres agreed. "Yes, sir."

"That means discussions about the case must be in controlled locations and only with people involved in the investigation. Also, do not share information from one segment, say the autopsy, with another segment, such as forensics."

Jason couldn't remember a time when he been given such a restrictive set of guidelines. Then again, he couldn't remember a fellow detective being in a similar situation before, either. Torres had so far barely said a word, but her face had remained grim. "It's pretty tough to do our job when we can't brainstorm with others."

Savage regarded her with an unblinking stare. "Find a way."

Sensing it was time to make their escape, Jason stood.

"We will, Lieutenant, we will."

Torres followed him back outside the office, and Jason immediately headed for the elevator. "See you in the morning, Dianna."

"Where are you going?"

Jason paused and turned to look at her. "Home. Where I'm going to keep my mouth shut."

Torres grinned. "Seems reasonable."

Jason laughed. "I thought so."

SHADOW OF DOUBT

Chapter 8

Jason's walk out to get the morning paper had become a chore. Every day there was something new on Rob Layne's murder, but none of the stories did anything to help the situation. Each story, many written by Devin James, seemed full of innuendo and inflammatory statements but contained very little in the way of facts.

Jason wondered if this had always been James's style, and Jason hadn't noticed it before, or if it was indeed a slander campaign as he suspected. Either way, picking up the paper was accompanied by a certain dread of what might be in it. On the other hand, he had to read it, so he could refute any blatant lies.

This morning, the front page had a picture of Lieutenant Savage standing before the press. Beneath were two more photos, one of Rob and the other of Vanessa. It occurred to him that not a single picture had been printed of Rob and Vanessa together.

Perhaps to make sure the public didn't get the impression they were once a happy family.

The heat wave was still going on, so Jason returned to the coolness of the house before unwrapping the newspaper. It was just a stall tactic.

San Antonio Police Release Statement
Department denies favoritism

(Devin James, Major Crimes Reporter)

At a late day press conference yesterday, Lieutenant Eric Savage of San Antonio Police Department's Homicide Division, issued a statement in reference to the Layne Body Shop murder that read in part:

"The truth will be sought out and the killer brought to justice. No favoritism…will be tolerated. All cases handled by this department will be thorough and fair, period."

This reporter attempted to ascertain through questioning if Detective Vanessa Layne was still the prime suspect in the case, or if the investigation had cleared Detective Layne. No response was given to our inquiries.

The full statement by the department can be read below.

Jason reached the limit of his patience. The statement had been edited to remove the idea that the press was responsible for a suggestion of favoritism, and James had declared Vanessa to be the prime suspect, at least at one time. He had no information to prove either claim.

Sandy was standing at the end of the hallway, coffee cup in hand, watching him. "More of the same?"

"Most definitely. I need to get Vanessa cleared, so the department can make it known to the public. Apparently, that's the only way I can put a stop to Devin's smear campaign."

"Whatever she did to piss him off, it's coming back to haunt her now."

Jason's cellphone started ringing from another room. He handed the paper to Sandy and went in search of the phone, eventually locating it in the family room. Whoever was on the other end had not given up.

He snatched up the phone. "Hello?"
"Jason?"
"Yes."

SHADOW OF DOUBT

"This is Sarah Morris."

"Hey, Captain. What's up?"

"The appeal hearing for Vanessa that was set for this morning…"

"Yeah."

"I've decided to delay it for a few days."

He wasn't sure which emotion he felt more—disappointed or surprised. Disappointment because he was aware Vanessa wanted the hearing over with, but there was little doubt that the timing was awful, especially considering the funeral was the next day. Surprise because of who he was talking to.

"I don't mean to step out of line, Captain, but does that mean you're the hearing officer for Vanessa's appeal?"

"That's correct."

To Jason, this was great news. No one could be fairer than Sarah Morris, and politics would have no part in her decision. "I wasn't aware."

"You weren't supposed to know, Jason. At least not until the hearing. This is an unusual situation."

"Yes, I guess it is. When will it be held?"

"A few days, maybe a week, after the funeral."

"Okay. Thanks for the call."

"You're welcome. Because of the appeal, I've had to limit my contact with Vanessa. How's she doing?"

"From what I can gather, she's holding up."

"There's nobody stronger."

Jason chuckled. "That seems to be the general sentiment."

"Bye, Jason. If I don't see you at the precinct, I'll see you at the funeral."

"Okay, Sarah. Bye."

He hung up to find Sandy watching him again. "You're starting to creep me out a little, always sneaking up on me."

She grinned at him. "Gotta make sure you're okay."

He kissed her. "I appreciate that."

****

Jason arrived at the precinct before Torres. With the hearing delayed, he opted to go straight to the station in the hopes that the phone records on Rob's cell had come in. He was rewarded with a thick folder laying on his desk.

After getting coffee, he sat down and started sorting through them. They went back thirty days, and it wasn't long before he picked up a couple numbers that were unfamiliar but reoccurred repeatedly. He dialed the first one.

"Thank you for calling NAPA auto parts. How can I help you?"

"Nothing, thanks. I need to redial."

"Okay."

He hung up and dialed the other number. A female answered.

"Hello?"

"Yes, this is Detective Jason Strong with the San Antonio PD. Who am I speaking with?"

"Patricia."

"Patricia?"

"Patricia Carlos. What is this about?"

"Ma'am, your phone number has come up in an investigation. I would like to speak with you if that would be possible."

"What sort of an investigation, Detective?"

"I'd rather not say at this time. When could we meet?"

An extended pause. "Does this have to do with Rob Layne?"

"Yes, ma'am. It does."

Another pause. "Do you know where the Alamo Quarry Market is?"

"Sure, on Basse Road?"

"Yes. There's a Starbucks in the plaza. My husband sleeps during the day, so can we meet there around 10:00?"

Jason made a note. "That will be fine. How will I know you?"

"Order a coffee and give your name, I'll be listening."

"Okay. I'll have my partner with me. See you then."

She hung up without saying goodbye.

"Who was that?"

Jason looked up to see Torres had arrived. "Patricia Carlos."

"I repeat, who was that?"

"If my hunch is right, she's Rob Layne's mistress."

Torres settled into her chair. "No kidding? I guess the phone records came in."

"Yeah."

"So, when do we get to talk to Patricia Carlos?"

Jason looked at his watch. "10:00. Do you feel like going to Starbucks?"

Torres grinned. "Sure. Are you buying?"

"Nope. The department is. That's where we're meeting Miss Carlos."

****

Between the Olmos Basin Golf Club on the west and the Quarry Golf Club on the east is the sprawling complex known as the

SHADOW OF DOUBT

Alamo Quarry Market. The huge, open-air shopping mall consisted of multiple structures spread over thirteen-plus acres in north-central San Antonio.

High-end retailers such as *Ann Taylor, Nordstrom's,* and *Kay Jewelers* shared space alongside lesser-known shops with names like *Calico Corners* and *Woodhouse Day Spa.* In addition, over a dozen restaurants supplied shoppers with multiple options for food and beverage. *Starbuck's Coffee* shared a large building with *Pottery Barn* and faced the exterior of the mall.

Jason, with Torres in tow, pulled up just before 10:00. They entered the restaurant, and though the tables were crowded, the line to order was short. A barista named Kurt greeted them.

"What'll be?"

Jason looked up at the menu briefly but opted for his usual. "Mocha Latte."

"What size?"

"Grande, please."

"Whipped cream?"

Jason smiled. "Definitely."

Torres chimed in from behind him. "Make it two."

Kurt added the second one. "Perfect. Name?"

"Jason."

After watching his name scrawled on the coffee cups and paying the bill, Jason moved down to the end of the counter, where both he and Torres scanned the room. Jason didn't notice a female customer who seemed overly interested in them, but even though they weren't wearing their badges on their chests, Jason had no doubt they would be picked out as cops.

"Order for Jason!"

Two cups sat on the counter, clear lids revealing a small mountain of whipped cream. They each retrieved one. When they turned around to scan for a table, a woman immediately to their right lifted her hand.

"Won't you join me?"

"Patricia?"

"Yes."

Jason and Dianna each pulled out a chair. Jason pulled out his badge.

"I'm Detective Strong, and this is my partner, Detective Torres."

The woman, who Jason guessed to be in her early thirties, had the same jet-black hair as Vanessa. That, however, was where the similarities ended. Her Spanish heritage shone through her brown eyes and smooth skin, and the dress she wore was far too feminine for Vanessa.

She gave them a weak smile. "Thank you for meeting me here."

"It was no problem. Thank you for meeting with us."

"I saw the news about Robby's murder. I was shocked."

For a moment, Jason's brain short-circuited. He'd never heard his friend referred to as *Robby*. "How long have you known…Robby?"

"About a year."

"How did you meet?"

"He did some work on my car. I was in an accident, and the insurance company recommended him."

"And you became friends?"

Her gaze moved down to the cup in front of her. "Yes."

Torres was writing furiously. "Miss Carlos, were you and Mr. Layne romantically involved?"

"Yes."

"How long?"

"About six months."

Jason's thoughts went to his dead friend.

How could he do that to Vanessa? She adored him. They had a son together and a good life.

He wanted to be angry with Rob, to blame him for his own death, but that would be stupid. Even if he had cheated, and even if it did lead to his death, he hadn't deserved to be murdered. It takes two to make a marriage and usually two to end one.

"Mrs. Carlos, do you know if Mr. Layne had revealed your relationship to Mrs. Layne?"

"I don't know. He never said he had."

"When was the last time you saw Mr. Layne?"

"The night before he was killed."

"Where did you see him?"

"At his shop."

Jason sipped his coffee, but Torres was ignoring hers, instead furiously writing notes since she'd sat down. She paused and looked up at Patricia Carlos. "Did Mr. Carlos know about the affair?"

Now focused on the floor beneath her feet, she managed an almost imperceptible nod. "He found out last week."

"I gather he wasn't pleased."

"No. I promised to end it, and that is why I visited Robby at his shop the night before his death."

"Did your husband know you were going there?"

"Yes, but he had to work."

Jason sipped the last of his coffee. "Where does your husband work?"

"He's a deputy with the Bexar County sheriff's office."

SHADOW OF DOUBT

Jason and Torres stared at each other, neither of them speaking for a moment. The fact Mr. Carlos was a deputy was both startling and alarming. Jason's mind reeled at the implications.

There's a good chance the deputy carried a 9 millimeter handgun. He would also be proficient with it.

Then there were the ramifications of a police officer who shot another officer's husband because the two non-law-enforcement spouses were having an affair. It took the concept of a sordid news story to unprecedented heights.

Jason noticed tears welling up in Patricia's eyes. "What is your husband's name?"

"Eddy…Edward Carlos."

"Could he have followed you to Rob's shop on the night you went to break things off?"

She looked up now, fear spreading across her face as she obviously inferred the meaning behind Jason's question. "I…I don't think so. He was on duty."

"Mrs. Carlos, where were you on the night Rob Layne was murdered?"

She began to tremble. "I was home with Eddy."

"So… Both you and your husband were home that night?"

She nodded.

"Was anyone else there?"

"No."

"What about visitors?"

"No…no one."

Torres was flipping pages and scribbling frantically in an obvious effort to keep up with Jason's questioning. When he fell silent, she sat with her pen poised over the notepad.

Jason handed a napkin to the woman, who wiped at her tears.

He turned to Torres. "You have any other questions?"

Torres shook her head.

Jason stood. "Thank you for your time, Mrs. Carlos."

Shaken, she seemed unable to respond. Jason couldn't be sure she even noticed they'd left the table.

****

Jason and Dianna stopped back at the precinct to speak with Lieutenant Savage. They needed to interview Deputy Carlos, but walking into a sister department and demanding to question a fellow officer was not likely to foster good relations, and Jason wanted somebody higher up to smooth the way. Because the lieutenant was relatively new to the department and didn't have anything in the way of connections at the sheriff's office, Savage called up to Captain Morris.

They were sitting in Savage's office when he punched the speaker button. "Captain, we have a bit of a situation."

"Another one?"

"Well, yes and no."

"I'm busy, Eric. Get to it."

"Yes, ma'am. I'll let Jason explain."

"Afternoon, Captain."

"Hi, Jason. Shoot."

Jason spent the next six or seven minutes explaining their predicament. When he was done, all three sat quietly, waiting for the captain's response.

After a long silence, she sighed. "Hold on."

The line clicked when she put them on hold. While he waited, noticed they suddenly didn't have anything to say to each other. They stared at their hands, and waited. Shortly, the speaker came alive again.

"Jason?"

"I'm here."

"See Captain Erlichman. He'll be expecting you."

"Yes, ma'am."

"Is that all, Eric?"

"That's it, Captain."

"We'll talk later then. Goodbye."

The phone clicked off, and Savage hung up his end. "You have your contact. Better get on it."

****

A large complex on the west side of the city, the Bexar County Sheriff's Office and Detention Center stretched nearly five city blocks. The multi-colored brick structure was home to the sheriff's office and its jail.

At the front entrance, a serious deputy greeted them. "How can I help you?"

Jason showed his badge. "Detective Strong. Can you tell me where I can find Captain Erlichman?"

"Sure. He should be in his office. Take that hallway back to the patrol division, and ask at the desk."

"Thanks."

Jason and Torres followed the instructions until they came upon a female deputy at the patrol desk. Jason still had his badge out.

"Detectives Strong and Torres to see Captain Erlichman."

SHADOW OF DOUBT

The noticeably overweight, auburn-haired deputy slid out of her chair with some effort and went back to an office. "Cap, a couple detectives from city are here to see you."

She turned and headed back to them, followed by the captain.

Erlichman was tall, easily over six-six, and lanky. His stride was long and his smile easy. "Jason?"

"Yes, sir."

A long arm and strong hand extended toward him, and they shook. "Good to meet you. Don Erlichman."

"Nice to meet you. This is my partner, Detective Dianna Torres."

They shook hands. "Pleasure to meet you, Dianna. Is it all right if I call you Dianna?"

"Of course. Thank you for seeing us."

"Nothing to it. Anything for Sarah. She and I go all the way back to the academy. Follow me."

Jason and Torres trailed the captain into his office, where he pointed at two metal folding chairs. "Take a seat."

The office was better described as a cubicle with a door, and both Jason and Torres found their knees pressed against the front of the captain's desk. Erlichman closed the door and moved around to the other side.

"Now, Sarah said you had a delicate situation and asked me to help. What, exactly, are we talking about?"

Jason had hoped Sarah would have laid out some of the background already, but apparently not. He opted to start at the beginning.

"Sir, the murder of a local business man turned out to be tied to one of our detectives."

"Vanessa Layne, correct?"

He's been reading the papers.

"Yes, sir. During our investigation, we've discovered that the victim was having an affair."

Erlichman shook his head. "Got caught with his hand in the cookie jar and paid for it, is that what you're thinking?"

Jason shrugged. "It's one possibility. We found the woman in question and spoke with her. Her name is Patricia Carlos."

The smile disappeared from the captain's face. "Carlos?"

"Yes, sir. She's the wife of one of your deputies."

"Eddy Carlos?"

"Yes, sir."

"Son of a castrated buck! Poor Eddy. What do you need from me?"

Jason leaned forward, lowering his voice, even though the door was closed.

"Sir, Deputy Carlos only learned about the affair last week, just days before the victim was killed."

The captain's gaze scanned from Jason to Dianna and back again. "Are you telling me my deputy is a suspect?"

"Person of interest would be more accurate."

"What else do you have to connect him?"

"That's why we're here. We would like to interview him."

Erlichman stared hard at Jason, his intensity having an almost physical impact.

After what seemed like minutes but was probably seconds, the captain stood up. "Wait here."

He left the room, and Jason turned to look at Dianna. "What do you think?"

"Nice guy, right up until you threatened one of his deputies."

"I didn't threaten!"

"Okay, suggested impropriety."

"That I did."

Erlichman returned, standing by the door. "Detectives, please follow me."

They got up and trailed the captain, whose steps were twice as long as theirs, out the door and down the hall. They finally caught up with him outside an interview room.

"If you two will make yourselves at home, I'll get Deputy Carlos."

Jason nodded. "Thank you."

They went into the room, which was equipped with the standard table and three chairs, a camera in the corner, and a one-way mirror. Jason figured the camera would be rolling, not to help them but to watch out for Eddy Carlos.

Less than two minutes later, the door opened.

Deputy Edward Carlos introduced himself and shook hands with both Jason and Torres. His dark skin and wide eyes were handsome, and despite being at least a foot shorter than his boss, his grip was equally firm.

"Cap says you wanted to talk to me about my wife."

This time, Torres took the lead. "Yes. It's about her connection to a murder case we're working."

"Rob Layne?"

"Yes."

"I didn't have nothing to do with it, and neither did she."

"We know you learned your wife was having an affair with Mr. Layne."

"Yeah, and she broke it off. I didn't need to kill him."

SHADOW OF DOUBT

Jason picked up very little in the way of tension coming from the man. "Deputy, would you show us your service weapon?"

Carlos stared at Jason for a minute then shrugged. Unsnapping his holster, he laid a 9 millimeter Glock 17 on the table.

Jason took note of the caliber but didn't touch the gun. "Where were you on the night Mr. Layne was killed?"

"With my wife at home. We were there all night."

"Is there anyone who can verify that?"

"No. We needed time alone. As you can imagine, we had some things to talk about."

"Do you own any other guns?"

"Sure. A Colt .45 and a Beretta .32"

Jason pointed toward the gun on the table. "We would like to take your gun for ballistic testing."

"I don't think so!"

"Why not?"

"I need it for my shift tonight."

Just then, the door opened again. This time, Captain Erlichman was standing there. "Let them have it, Eddy."

"But, sir—"

"You heard me." He looked at Jason. "Are you done here, Detective?"

"I believe so."

"Good. See yourselves out, will you? Eddy, you're with me."

Everyone stood, and Torres produced an evidence bag for the gun. Jason put on gloves, removed the clip, popped the chamber round, then dropped all of it into the bag. The captain and his deputy were already gone.

****

Despite it being late in the day by the time they made it back to the precinct, they found Doc Josie still in her lab, staring through a microscope. Jason dropped the gun on the steel table next to her. The echoing twang startled the department head, and she bolted away from the scope.

"Dear Lord, Jason. You scared the crap out of me."

"Sorry, Doc."

She eyed him suspiciously. "I bet."

"No, really. I was just saying to Dianna that I hoped I didn't startle you."

Josie looked at Torres. "Did he?"

"Not that I recall."

"That's what I thought!"

Jason lifted the gun back off the table. "Here, I'll hand it to you nicely. Can you test fire this and compare it against the Layne projectiles?"

"Sure. Probably be tomorrow before I get it done though."

"That's fine. Oh, by the way, are you going to the funeral?"

Josie nodded. "Of course."

"See you there."

Jason and Torres headed back up to the third floor. Lieutenant Savage was waiting for them. "How did it go?"

Jason shrugged. "Okay. We had a chance to talk with him, and we got his firearm for testing."

"Did you learn anything new?"

"Not really. His alibi is the same as his wife's, which is they were home together all night."

Torres ripped a piece of paper from her pad. "Those are both of the Carlos's phone numbers. Can you get the records for us?"

Savage took the paper. "Sure. What's next?"

Jason sighed. "The funeral."

Savage closed his eyes. "Yeah, I forgot. Tomorrow morning, right?"

"Yes, sir."

"Then you two need to get home and get some rest. Tomorrow will not be an easy day."

John C. Dalglish

Chapter 9

A driving rain announced the end of the suffocating heat. The first cool front of the year came through overnight, and with it heavy downpours. Jason pushed himself out of bed and crossed the room to look out the window. A steady, morning drizzle had replaced the night's hard rain, and the searing blue sky of the heat wave had been replaced by gray, ominous clouds.

It seemed fitting and certainly matched his mood, considering what lay ahead. Rob's funeral would be a temporary break from his quest to clear his partner, but it would not serve as a respite from the stress of the past few days or from the pressure that was sure to come in the weeks ahead.

Sandy had been first to rise, and the aroma of fresh coffee reached him. Throwing on a robe and slippers, he made his way down to the kitchen.

She was just finishing some scrambled eggs. "Hungry?"

"Yes and no."

She smiled as she carried the pan over to his plate and dumped a large helping in front of him. "I'm the same way, but we're gonna need something in us."

"I suppose. Where are the kids?"

"Family room. I told them you would come in and say good morning."

He left his eggs untouched and went in to see them. Nina was sprawled on the couch and David on the floor. Penny was standing outside the back door with her nose pressed against the glass. The TV was showing their favorite cartoon, SpongeBob Squarepants. He bent over and kissed his daughter on the top of her head.

"Morning, Pumpkin."

"Morning, Dad."

David rolled over and threw himself onto Jason. "Daddy!"

Jason held him close and brushed at his son's hair, attempting to smooth a patch that refused to lay down. "Morning, Champ. How's my buddy?"

"Good."

Jason set him back on the floor. "Enjoy your show. I'm gonna eat breakfast."

Returning to the kitchen, Jason found a piece of buttered toast keeping his eggs company. He sat down and attempted to eat.

Sandy sat across from him, her pink pajamas and matching robe hanging loosely from her shoulders. She cradled her coffee in two hands, her gaze penetrating the steam from her cup and fixing on him.

"I'm taking the kids to a sitter. Do you want me to meet you at the funeral home?"

He washed down some eggs with his coffee. "That's up to you. I plan on being early, so if you don't care about that, then we can drop off the kids and go together."

"That sounds good. What time will we leave?"

Jason looked up at the wall clock, a retro-looking star design that Sandy kept because it reminded her of her mother. "It's almost 7:00. I want to leave no later than 8:15."

Sandy pushed herself up from the table. "In that case, I'd better get moving."

****

Pulling up at the single-story brownstone structure, the arrival at Colonial Funeral Home turned out to be a somewhat surreal experience. The drizzle had turned back to rain, not unlike the day John Patton was laid to rest, and a sense of déjà vu was impossible to miss.

Sandy was in the same outfit she'd worn that day—black slacks, black shoes, and a dark-gray blouse. His clothes were also the same as that sad day not so long ago. Even the awning over the entrance flapped in the same lazy way as the last time, and the faces of the people under it bore the same somber look.

He and Sandy were among the first to arrive, passing a couple TV news crews setting up at the edge of the parking lot. SAPD had erected a portable barrier across the entrance to the lot and was checking everyone they let in.

Within the funeral home, Jason found the pattern of familiarity continued. The same low lighting, padded pews, and dark carpet guided his eyes to the front. There, on the same low table that had once held John's casket, was Rob's coffin. Like at the captain's visitation, the casket was closed, but unlike John Patton's, there was no American flag draped over it.

Vanessa had asked Jason what he thought about the casket being closed. She felt like it would be traumatic for Kasen to see his daddy lying there, but unable to answer his questions. Jason had agreed.

Perhaps he should have expected to be struck by the sense of history repeating itself; after all, most funerals were somewhat similar. Nevertheless, he struggled not to relive the emotions of the captain's death all over again, instead trying to focus on the loss of his friend. It wasn't easy.

Once inside, they went in search of Vanessa and found her sitting in the front row with Kasen and Rachel. Sandy kneeled down in front of Vanessa and gave her a hug. "Hey. How are you holding up?"

Vanessa shrugged. "I'm taking it a day at a time."

Kasen noticed his Uncle Jason and climbed out of his aunt's arms. "Uncle Jason!"

Jason gathered the boy up and held him tight. He had the eyes and hair of his father but the spirit of his mother. "Hey, Kasen. Are you taking care of your mom?"

"Yeah. She's crying a lot, though."

Jason looked down at his friend and partner, who managed a smile for her son. Vanessa held out her arms, and Jason placed Kasen in her lap. She brushed at the boy's hair.

"He's been a really big boy. I'm very proud of him."

SHADOW OF DOUBT

Jason caught Sandy's eye and gestured toward the door. She nodded, and he slipped away.

Back at the door, a steady stream of mourners was beginning to arrive. Jason stood off to the side, an umbrella over him, and watched for anyone unusual. It would not be the first time the murderer attended a victim's funeral. So far, he recognized most of the people coming in out of the rain.

Lieutenant Savage went by, tipping his head but not stopping, as did Torres. Captain Morris and Gavin did stop to talk briefly, and when Jason turned back to the parking lot, he spotted a familiar face holding up the line at the barricade.

Jason dropped his umbrella and took off at a dead run. The guard was just about to let the man through when Jason stepped in front of the sedan, his badge held up for the officer to see. "This man is not welcome at the funeral."

The officer looked at Jason, then at the man in the car. "You heard him, sir. I can't let you in."

Jason came around to the driver's window. "Your presence is not appreciated here, James."

"Come on, Jason. I've known Vanessa for years."

"I couldn't give a rip! You're no friend to her or her family."

Jason turned to the officer. "This man is not to be allowed in, and if he attempts to come in again, arrest him for creating a disturbance."

"Yes, sir."

Jason left the newsman sitting there and walked back to the entranceway. By now, he was soaked from the rain. He didn't care.

Back inside, he sat down next to Sandy as the service was about begin.

She leaned over. "What happened to you?"

"I needed to clarify the attendance policy for someone."

"Oh, who?"

"Devin James."

"Ah. I see."

Jason's thoughts seesawed between the service and his efforts to clear Vanessa. In truth, he'd found it easier to focus on the case than what was going on around him. The distraction of the investigation was a kind of defense mechanism.

SHADOW OF DOUBT

When the funeral service was over, Jason had been one of the first to the door and made sure no press attempted to ask questions of the mourners. He understood the media's need to chronicle the service from a visual standpoint, but he wouldn't tolerate questions being hurled at mourners who had just gone through a funeral.

It turned out he needn't have worried.

The TV crews had their shots and were gone, and even Devin James had made himself scarce. Sandy was one of the last to the door, with Vanessa and Kasen in tow.

Jason hugged his partner. "It was beautiful, Vanessa."

"It was, wasn't it?"

Kasen had fallen silent, the mood around him seeming to have taken its toll.

Jason looked at Sandy then at Vanessa. "Are we taking you guys home?"

Vanessa shook her head. "No, but thanks. Rachel is driving us."

Jason popped open the umbrella for himself and Sandy. "Okay. We're going to pick up the kids, then we'll see you there."

Back in the car, the rain showed no sign of letting up as they drove toward the sitters. Only the repetitive back and forth of the windshield wipers broke the silence.

When Sandy finally spoke, her question surprised him.

"Will you be able to clear Vanessa?"

The surprise on his face turned to a scowl. "Of course. Why would you ask such a thing?"

"I don't know. You've been working hard on it, but you don't seem to be making any headway."

Irritation crept into his voice. "She didn't do it, Sandy. Therefore, I'll be able to clear her."

"I didn't say she did it. I wouldn't believe it was possible, either."

He glanced at her, suspicion oozing from his tone. "Wouldn't or couldn't?"

"What do you mean?"

"You said, *wouldn't believe it.* That's not the same as *couldn't*. It implies you think she may have."

"Don't put words in my mouth, Jason." Sandy was now on the defensive. "You know very well how I feel about Vanessa."

He stared straight ahead, suddenly mesmerized by the rain. "It's not possible she killed Rob, okay?"

Sandy turned to the side window. "Okay, but it scares me."

"What does?"

"Being in the same position. The thought of what I might do."

"I'm not following."

"If I found out you cheated on me…I just don't know."

Jason's mouth was hanging open. "You could shoot me?"

"Probably not."

"*Probably* not!"

She turned back to him, a slightly mischievous smile playing at the corner of her mouth. "Well, for starters, I don't own a gun."

"Well, thank goodness for that! And just so we're clear, there is no reason for you to need a gun."

"I know that." The smile disappeared. "All I'm saying is that people do things *you* never expected when confronted with a situation *they* never expected."

He looked over at her then back at the rain-soaked road. After a long pause to consider her words, he nodded. "Point taken."

****

The next morning, Jason arrived at the precinct to find no sign of Torres, but a note was waiting for him on his desk.

Went down to check on ballistics of Carlos gun. DT.

"Detective Strong?"

Jason turned to see Deputy Carlos standing behind him. "Deputy, I didn't see you there. What can I do for you?"

"I got a call from your partner saying I could pick up my gun."

"Oh…well…I wasn't aware she'd called you."

"Does that mean you don't have my gun?"

Over the deputy's shoulder, Jason saw the elevator doors open, and Torres step out carrying the bag with the gun.

He pointed behind the deputy. "I suspect that's it there."

Carlos turned to see Torres walking toward him with her arm outstretched. "Here you go, Deputy. I appreciate your cooperation."

Carlos accepted the bag, removed the gun and clip, then tossed the bag on Jason's desk. He checked the chamber, loaded the clip, and put the gun in his holster. "Thanks."

"I appreciate you coming by to pick it up."

"No problem. See you later."

They watched him get on the elevator and the doors close.

Torres turned to Jason. "Not a match. His gun wasn't used in the homicide."

"So I gathered."

"Now we can look at his phone records. If they back up his story, then I think we can rule out both he and his wife."

Jason looked at his desk. "Did they come in?"

"Yes. I thought we might take them into the conference room. There's something else, too."

"What's that?"

"While I was downstairs, Doc Josie asked if I wanted the ledger from the shop. She had finished processing it, and Rob Layne was the only one whose fingerprints were found on it."

"So you have it?"

"Yes. I thought we should go over it and look for anyone who might have owed money to him."

"Sounds good. I'm gonna get some coffee. Meet you in there?"

"Okay."

Just a few minutes later, they both had phone records in front of them, highlighting markers at the ready. They were only interested in the night of Rob's death. If the Carlos couple was at home, then they weren't the killers.

Jason was focused on the records of Patricia Carlos while Torres was pouring over the husband's logs. Without looking up, she broke the concentrated silence of the room.

"How are you makin' it, Jason?"

"Nothing so far."

"No, I mean how are *you* doing? The funeral was pretty rough."

He leaned back. "I'll make it. I keep emotionally swaying back and forth. One minute I'm grieving the loss of my friend, the next I'm worried about clearing Vanessa."

Torres was watching him now. "It can take a toll, that's for sure."

"Yeah. I remember back when John passed away, it seemed I operated on some sort of autopilot. It was easier to push emotion aside at the time."

"You eventually have to deal with it. Things like this can eat you alive."

He nodded. "I know. Eventually, I had to take a few days off. Only then was I able to get my bearings again."

"Well, I'm here if you need anything."

"I appreciate that. Right now, I want to focus on finding the killer."

Silence fell over the room again as they both continued their search. After another twenty minutes or so, Jason put the cap back on his highlighter.

"Patricia's phone never left her residence that night. If she was involved, she left her cellphone at home."

Torres pushed her sheets away from her. "Same here. While it's not impossible that he did it, I find it unlikely they were in it together, and she's covering for him."

"It's possible."

"Sure, if she was afraid of her husband, perhaps. But we've got nothing to suggest that's the case. And with his gun not being a match, it gets hard to argue they should be suspects."

Jason wasn't ready to give up. "We need to interview the neighbors. Find out if anyone saw them leave that night."

"Good idea. You go over the ledger, and see if you can find someone of interest to check out. I'll do the neighborhood canvas."

"So if I don't find a suspect in the ledger, and a neighbor vouches for the Carlos couple, what are we left with?"

Torres avoided his eyes. "Not what, who. It only leaves Vanessa."

Jason stared at her, his conviction wavering slightly. "Do you really think she could have done it?"

"As I said before, I don't know her as well as you do. I'm just following the evidence. Right now, my gut says she did it."

He figured Torres had pinned Vanessa as guilty all along, but this was the first time she'd come out and said it. He shook his head back and forth emphatically.

"I'm not convinced."

She shrugged. "I understand. It's a circumstantial case, and those can be interpreted in more than one way, but I doubt it'll be our call, anyway."

He agreed with her there. Any decision to arrest Vanessa would at least come from the lieutenant and probably from above him. In fact, the district attorney, who would have to prosecute the case, would probably make the final determination to issue a warrant or not.

The decision to arrest a suspect didn't usually have to go that far up the chain of command, but cases involving officers were a whole different animal.

Torres started gathering her papers. "We should tell Savage, I guess."

****

Lieutenant Savage was not in his office, but they found him by the coffee machine.

Jason held out his cup for Savage to fill it. "Thanks."

Savage grinned. "Don't get used to it."

Jason forced a smile, despite his mood. "We need to talk."

The lieutenant looked at him, then Torres, then back at him. "You and me, or all three of us?"

"All three."

"Okay then. My office."

They followed him, Torres carrying a file folder with her. Once inside and seated, she put the folder on the lieutenant's desk.

"Those are the phone records of both Patricia and Eddy Carlos. They support their story of being at home on the night Rob Layne was killed."

Savage stared at the folder but did not open it. "What about the ballistics on the gun?"

"Not a match. If Eddy killed him, he didn't do it with his service weapon."

"Okay, so where does that leave us?"

"I'm going to do a canvas of the neighborhood where Mr. and Mrs. Carlos live to see if we can find someone who will vouch for them being home. Jason is going to go over the financial ledger to see if someone had a bad business dealing with the victim."

"And if neither of those pans out, where will we be?"

A momentary silence dropped over the room like a wet blanket on a fire. Only a few wisps of smoke escaped to indicate what lay beneath the surface. Finally, Torres said it.

"We'll be left with only one suspect. Vanessa."

Savage looked at Jason, who had remained quiet. "You agree?"

"Do I agree she would be our only suspect remaining…yes."

The lieutenant leaned back in his chair and stared up at the ceiling. "So you two want to know what you should do then. Is that it?"

Neither Jason nor Torres answered the rhetorical question. Jason stared at the floor, unsure what to expect.

Savage let out a sigh. "What would we normally do with a suspect in that situation?"

Jason looked up. "We've never been in a situation like this; at least I haven't."

"That's not what I mean. Suppose the suspect was not Vanessa but instead Patricia Carlos. What would we do?"

"I guess we'd ask her to take a polygraph."

"Then since we're doing this by the book, let's do what we would with anyone else. Ask Vanessa Layne to take a polygraph."

Torres fidgeted in her seat. "Should we wait until we've cleared the other suspects?"

"You two are in here because you expect that to happen, right?"

Jason and Torres nodded.

Torres shifted again. "When should we schedule it?"

"Not today. Too close to the funeral. Tomorrow morning if possible."

Jason stood and moved to the door. "I'll do the call to let her know."

Torres nodded. "Of course."

Jason looked at his boss. "Are we done here, Lieutenant?"

"I am."

"Excuse me then; I've got a call to make."

****

Vanessa checked the time. 11:30.

Sitting on the couch, the TV showing cartoons for Kasen, she found herself surprised to look down and see she was still in her pajamas. Then she found it surprising she was surprised. In fact, she'd changed into them right after Jason and Sandy had left the previous night, and there didn't seem to be a good reason to get out of them for the day.

She was keeping Kasen home, she didn't have to go to work, and nobody else was expected to come by. With no desire to fight the sadness enveloping her, it seemed logical to assume she would probably still be dressed for bed when and if sleep came later that night. So far, it had been elusive.

The ringing phone startled her back to the present. Without getting up, she reached across the couch and picked up her cell.

"Hello?"

"Vanessa, it's Jason."

"Hey."

"How ya doin'?"

"Been better."

"No doubt. How's Kasen doing?"

She looked down at her son, also still in his pajamas and sprawled on the floor in front of the TV. "You know how kids are. He seems to be doing better than I am, but sometimes, there's a volcano beneath the surface that they don't know how to release."

"He's an amazing kid."

"That he is."

When Jason hesitated for just a second, she detected it immediately. "That's not why you called, is it?"

"Why do you say that?"

"Don't answer my question with one of your own. It's annoying."

"Well...I did call to check on you, but there is something else."

"Spill it, Jason."

Kasen rolled over and stared at her. "Is that Uncle Jason?"

"Yes. Do you want to say hi?"

Kasen bobbed his head, and Vanessa punched the speaker button.

"Go ahead."

"Hi, Uncle Jason!"

"Hey, Kasen. Whatcha doin'?"

"Watchin' TV. Are you coming over?"

"Not today, but you can come visit me and Aunt Sandy for a sleepover soon. How's that?"

"Super."

Vanessa grinned at her son. "Say goodbye."

"Bye, Uncle Jason."

She took the phone off speaker and put it back to her ear. "It means so much to him when he hears your voice."

Jason cleared his throat. "So...the other reason I called. It's to ask you if you'd come down to the station for a poly."

"You want me to take a poly exam? Why?"

"It wasn't my idea, but Savage says we have to treat you like any other suspect…person of interest."

Her heart skipped a beat. "You said suspect. Is that what I am?"

"We've looked into a lot of people, Vanessa."

"How many of them have taken a polygraph?"

His silence told her what she already knew. Anger crept into her voice. "I didn't kill Rob!"

"I believe you, Vanessa, I do. But it's not up to me, and I figured you'd rather I called than someone else."

"Like who?"

"Don't go there, okay. Just come down, do the test, and never look back."

She wanted to raise a stink but wasn't sure what the impact would be. It could just make her look guilty. In fact, she wasn't sure about anything anymore.

Her exhaustion won out. "When?"

"Tomorrow morning? Say 9:00?"

"Fine. I'll be there."

"Good. Don't worry about it, okay? Just get it over with."

"That's easy for you to say!"

He paused for a long time. When he did speak, it was barely above a whisper. "I'm sorry."

Tears filled her eyes for the hundredth time. "No, I am. I know you're just doing what you have to do. I'm glad you were the one who called."

"See you in the morning?"

"Yeah. Bye."

She hung up and wiped her eyes. Kasen hadn't noticed the tears this time, and she wanted to keep it that way. He'd seen enough adults crying in the last week to last a lifetime.

When her eyes were dry, she reached down and tickled his foot. "How about some pizza?"

"Yummy!"

"Then pizza it is."

John C. Dalglish

Chapter 10

Tony Moreno had been a polygraph examiner for over three decades. Born in a small town along the Texas-Mexico border, his career in law enforcement had brought him out of a rough childhood, and his pride in the job was obvious. At just five-foot-four and a hundred and eighty pounds, he often described his physique as square. He liked to say that if he fell onto his side, he'd be the same height as when he was standing up.

This easy-going nature allowed people to focus on the questions rather than the examiner. While notoriously unreliable, polygraphs were still used to get a read on possible suspects, and Tony was one of the best in the business.

Just before nine in the morning, he arrived and set up his equipment in the conference room. Only one exam was on his agenda, but it would be as difficult a test as he had ever run. Vanessa Layne was a colleague and friend, which caused him to consider disqualifying himself as the examiner, but Jason had insisted.

"We need you to do this, Tony. You're the only one I trust, and Vanessa feels the same way."

He'd agreed, as much as because they asked, as because he wanted to be sure the test was done correctly. The only way to do that was to conduct it himself.

At nine sharp, Vanessa tapped on the door.

Tony looked up and smiled. "Come in, Vanessa."

Because the heat had not yet returned, she was dressed in jeans and a long-sleeve shirt. She looked better than he'd expected.

"Hi, Tony."

"If you're ready, then take a seat there."

She did, lowering herself into the chair as if it might explode. "Thanks for doing this."

"Of course." He went around in front of her so she could see his face. "Look, just answer the questions without thinking too much, and the truth will take care of itself. You'll be done shortly, and this can be over."

She nodded as he started to hook her up to the machine. First, he wrapped a blood pressure cuff around her arm. Next, he placed two elaborate rubber tubes around her body, one at chest level, and the other on the abdomen.

Finally, he attached a pair of electrodes onto two of her fingers. "Now I know you are familiar with the tests, but I have to go over a few things, regardless."

Again, she nodded but didn't speak.

"First, you have the blood pressure cuff, used for the obvious. Second, the pneumographs around your torso, which measure your respiratory rate. And lastly, the galvanometers, which are attached to your fingers. They measure electro-dermal activity."

Vanessa's forehead furrowed, drawing a smile from Tony.

"Sorry…sweat gland activity."

She nodded.

Tony played with some knobs, turned on a couple switches, then took a seat behind her.

"Okay, Vanessa, I'm going to ask you some basic questions. Easy stuff just to get a baseline level. Ready?"

Another nod, one last button push, and the machine began to make a soft whirring noise. Tony's voice dropped into a long, practiced monotone.

"Is your name Vanessa Layne?"
"Yes."

****

Jason had made sure to be at the precinct before Vanessa. He didn't want her to feel as if she was alone. It turned out Torres wasn't in yet, either. Vanessa surprised him and everyone else by coming in looking refreshed. He couldn't imagine how she pulled it off, considering the last few days.

She looks better than I do, but then again, she normally does.

He smiled at his joke, briefly pushing aside some of his own nervousness. Despite her appearance, he knew Vanessa well enough that he had no trouble sensing the tension just below the surface, and something else, too. Fear.

It was easy to understand why. If the test didn't go well, especially if she failed completely, it would be very hard for her to convince even her friends that she was innocent. Those who suspected her already and those on the fence would be hard-pressed not to arrest her. The lie detector wouldn't be admissible in court, but it could serve as the tipping point for a mostly circumstantial case.

Torres finally showed up at the precinct. "Hey, Jason. Is she in there?"

He nodded. "Yeah. What have you been up to?"

"I went over to the neighborhood of Eddy and Patricia Carlos. I found two people who recall seeing both of the Carlos's vehicles in the driveway all night."

Jason grunted. "I guess that takes them off the board now for sure. I didn't have any luck with the ledger. It was mostly names and phone numbers without any comments or notations."

"I was afraid of that. I'm going downstairs to get something to eat. You want anything?"

"No, thanks."

He looked up at the clock for the twentieth time. Vanessa had been in the room forty-five minutes. *It has to be finished soon.*

"I'm glad that's over."

He spun around to see Vanessa standing behind him. "You're finished?"

"Yes."

"How'd it go?"

She shrugged. "I guess all right. He didn't say I failed."

Jason had been hoping for a *No Deception Indicated* verdict. "So does that mean he gave you an NDI?"

"No. He said he needed to take another look at the graphs first."

Jason's chest tightened slightly. Not the ringing endorsement he'd hoped to hear. "Well, don't worry about it. I'll call you later after we see the report."

"Okay. Thanks."

As she got on the elevator, Tony came out of the conference room and disappeared into the lieutenant's office. The door closed behind him, leaving Jason to sit at his desk and wait. Torres hadn't returned yet.

Less than ten minutes later, the office door opened again, and Tony reappeared. He avoided Jason's stare and went back to the conference room, presumably to pack up his equipment. Without coming to the door, Savage yelled for Jason.

At his desk, the lieutenant sat scowling down at some graph sheets, his mood and the atmosphere in the office both very dark. When he looked up, his eyes were blank, his expression guarded. "Where's Torres?"

"She went after some lunch."

Just then, she stuck her head through the door. "Did I hear my name?"

Savage signaled her in. "Shut the door."

She did, and she and Jason settled into chairs across from their boss.

Savage stabbed the graph paper in front of him. "This is the poly results."

Jason was tired of guessing. "And?"

"And Moreno graded it INC."

Jason wasn't sure if he was relieved or appalled. Inconclusive did nothing for Vanessa's plight. It didn't clear her, nor did it indict her. Truth was that most see an INC as leaning toward the determination that the person was lying, even though it did not strictly mean that.

Savage sucked in a long breath. "That reporter James is screaming cover-up in the papers almost daily. There's a lot of heat coming down from above, and the chief is being pressured to make a declaration on Vanessa."

Jason's chest tightened some more as the lieutenant got to the point.

"So...this is how we've been instructed to handle it. At 3:00 this afternoon, you two are to meet with Captain Morris, District Attorney Lusk, and myself. The meeting will be in the conference room and is to be structured this way."

He handed the polygraph sheets to Torres, who accepted them as if they were plague-ridden.

"Dianna, you will lay out the entire case *against* Detective Layne. You'll put it on the whiteboard, line by line, attempting to show that we should charge her."

Torres looked as if she might throw-up.

Savage turned to Jason. "You will then offer evidence that flies in the face of charging Detective Layne and why we should continue to look for other suspects."

It was Jason's turn to feel sick. He had to defend and protect his friend with no more than his belief that she couldn't have done it. A sinking feeling told him it wouldn't be enough.

Savage leaned back, his face maintaining a fixed neutrality.

"I'm not trying to pit the two of you against each other, and this isn't a contest. The captain and the D.A. want contrasting points of view. The final decision will come down not to who is more convincing, but to the facts presented. Don't try to color your comments with your personal convictions. As Joe Friday used to say—just the facts. Understood?"

Jason and Torres nodded.

"Good. You've got three hours to put together your briefs. Get to it."

****

Jason and Torres sat opposite each other, taking turns looking at the clock and making notes. The evidence they looked at was the same, but the interpretation was different. Where she accepted some of the details as 'circumstantial proof' of Vanessa's guilt, Jason looked at the same things as holes in the case.

The elephant in the room was the fact that more than a few killers had been convicted on circumstantial cases, many of which Jason himself had helped assemble. Throw in the fact that he was beginning to have his doubts, and he realized he had his work cut out for him.

"I'm going into the conference room."

He looked up to see Torres standing, notepad in hand. It was 2:45. "Okay. Is Savage in there already?"

She shook her head. "I'm gonna get the timeline laid out on the board before the meeting. I'd rather not try to do it and answer questions at the same time."

He felt a tinge of sympathy for her. It was a tough spot to be put in. Still new to the department, she now had to lay out why one of the most popular members of the SAPD should be arrested for murder.

Everyone in the room would be trying to shoot her down, including him, her new partner. "Probably a good idea. I'll see you in there."

His own notes were almost complete, but he would wait until 3:00 to go in. He was in no hurry to get started.

Only a few minutes later, District Attorney Lusk showed up and made his way to the lieutenant's office. Jason had met the D.A. several times before as a witness for the State in cases that Lusk was prosecuting. Jason liked and respected the man.

Known for three-piece suits and a pocket watch that made him look like an old-time barrister, the fiery redhead with a baritone voice had tempered some in recent years. Some of the red had been replaced by gray, and some of the fire had subsided under the political stresses of the job.

Still, he easily won another term during the last election, with one of his campaign promises being to fight any form of government corruption. A detective who committed a murder would certainly fall into that category, and Jason worried it spelled extra trouble for Vanessa.

While the door to Lieutenant Savage's office closed behind the D.A., the elevator doors opened to reveal Captain Morris. Her black hair was now tinged with gray, and the weight of recent events seemed to be taking their toll. Her smile, which had become ever-present since her wedding to Gavin, now seemed to come a little slower.

She stopped next to Jason and glanced toward the lieutenant's office. "Anyone in with Savage?"

"Yeah. Lusk just went in."

"Well, since I know what they're talking about, I'll just stay out here with you. How's the case look?"

Jason's face reflected his gloomy assessment. "Circumstantial but convincing. Especially because we don't have any other suspects."

The lieutenant's office door opened, and the two men emerged. Lusk and Savage both nodded at Morris as they headed for the conference room.

Sarah looked down at Jason. "Looks like it's show time."

She fell in line behind the two men, and Jason grabbed his notes and brought up the rear.

SHADOW OF DOUBT

John C. Dalglish

Chapter 11

The conference room was not large; in fact, *meeting* room would be a more appropriate title, since not much of a conference could be held there. A long table sat in the middle of the room, with anywhere from four to six chairs around it, depending on how many had been borrowed. A single telephone sat in the middle of the desk. White walls in need of fresh paint and a dry erase board hanging at the far end made up the rest of the room's interior.

Torres was standing next to the whiteboard, marker in hand, watching the group come in. On the board was a timeline, beginning at 4:30 on the day Rob Layne was killed. Lusk sat at the opposite end of the room from her, at the head of the table, with Savage on his right and Morris on his left. Jason took a seat near where Dianna stood and smiled at her in an attempt to give her some encouragement. Her eyes told him he'd failed.

SHADOW OF DOUBT

Jason studied the timeline, comparing it to his.

4:30 — DVL visits shooting range (stays until 6:00)
6:00 — DVL calls sister and asks her to keep son overnight
6:30 — DVL at home – makes phone call to garage.
11:00 — DVL makes phone call to garage
11:15 — DVL shows up at garage
11:30 — DVL leaves garage
11:30 - 12:15 — Rob Layne murdered – DVL seen leaving by witness
12:18 — First call to 911 – hang up.
12:30 — DVL finds body and calls 911

It all matched what Jason had.

When the settling into chairs was over and silence had fallen on the room, Lieutenant Savage nodded at Torres. She swallowed hard and started in.

"As you might have surmised, DVL refers to Detective Vanessa Layne. This is the timeline of events given to us by Detective Layne in her statement. We have verified, using phone records and interviews, all of it with one major exception. I'll get to that in a minute."

She flipped a page on her notes. "The early part of Detective Layne's day was not relevant, so I have not included it on the board. Suffice to say her whereabouts was accounted for and confirmed. The pertinent timeline starts with her visiting the firing range beginning at 4:30. Her presence there was verified."

Torres glanced up briefly, and with no questions coming, continued.

"When Detective Layne was asked about the trip to the range, she responded: 'It helps me. I can focus on shooting rather than things that are not going well elsewhere'."

Jason glanced toward Lusk. The fury of his note taking gave the word intense a whole new meaning.

Torres tapped the board at 6:00. "This is when Detective Layne contacted her sister and asked her to keep her son overnight. When I asked her why, she responded: 'Because I was hoping to see Rob'."

"Detective Layne then returned home and called her husband at the garage but got no answer."

Lusk stopped her. "The call to her husband's garage. Was it to a cell phone?"

Torres shook her head. "They were to the shop's phone. Detective Layne advised me that her husband did not use his cellphone while at work."

Lusk made a note then looked back at the board, waiting. Torres tapped 11:00.

"Between the phone call to the garage, which was on Detective Layne's phone records, and the next phone call to the garage at eleven in the evening, we do not have a verification of Detective Layne's whereabouts. There was a call to her sister around 8:30 that bounced off the tower near her home, and the phone continued pinging the same tower all evening."

She paused, taking a deep breath before continuing. Jason noted the tightening of her face muscles as she reached the critical part of the presentation, and watched her brace herself before starting.

"According to Detective Layne, she arrived at the body shop at 11:15. She claims to have gone inside, and after an exchange with her husband, left roughly fifteen minutes later. She then returns to the shop approximately an hour later to retrieve her cellphone, and finds her husband's body. At 12:30, the call to 9-1-1 comes in to the emergency services operator."

Lusk was sitting with his arms crossed, staring at the board. "This is the timeline according to Detective Layne's statement?"

"Yes, sir."

He looked at Morris then Savage. "Any questions?"

They both shook their head.

Lusk looked up at Torres. "Okay, now the case narrative."

Torres nodded, faced the table, flipped another page on her notes, and started in.

"It is my belief that Detective Layne visited the firing range in preparation for her planned attack on her husband. It served two purposes. One—she could make sure she was sharp with her weapon, and two—it would explain any traces of GSR that would be found on her clothes."

Lusk was apparently the only one who had questions. "Did you find GSR?"

"Yes, sir."

Torres waited for Lusk to make some notes then continued.

"Next, she contacted her sister with the request to keep her son overnight. This assured Detective Layne the freedom to come and go, as she needed. At 6:30, she attempted to contact Mr. Layne at the shop but was unsuccessful."

"Did anyone verify Detective Layne's presence at home? Did a neighbor or a friend see her?"

Torres shook her head. "The only evidence indicating she was at home is the pinging location of her phone."

"Which only proves her phone was there."

"Yes. There is also the call to her sister at 8:30, which only leaves a window of two and a half hours until the next call at 11:00, when she called the shop and a brief conversation took place. By Detective Layne's own admission, she then drove to the shop and spoke with her husband in person. An argument ensued, after which, Detective Layne acknowledges throwing her cellphone at her husband. She claims she then left in her car."

"Did Detective Layne say what the argument was about?"

"Yes. They'd been having marital problems for some time, and Rob Layne apparently had told her their marriage was over. He also revealed there was somebody else."

"Somebody else?"

"Another woman."

Jason caught the look exchanged between Savage and Morris. They weren't liking the evidence any more than he was

Lusk was focused strictly on Torres. "Did you confirm whether the other woman existed?"

"Yes. Her name was Patricia Carlos. We were able to speak with both her and her husband."

"The husband knew about the relationship?"

"He did. Apparently, he figured it out about a week before the murder. We were able to clear them both."

"How was that done?"

"The couple alibied each other, claiming they were home all night. Phone records and two neighbors confirmed it. Also, Edward Carlos is a Bexar County Sheriff's deputy, and was compelled to provide his gun for testing by his superior officer. Testing determined it was not a match for the murder weapon."

"So, you believe the fight and affair were the motive for the shooting?"

"Possibly. Because of Detective Layne's activities earlier in the day, I believe she may have been planning it all along."

"If she didn't know about the affair, then why would she be planning to kill him?"

Torres extracted a sheet of paper from the file in front of her and slid it to Lusk. "There was a one hundred thousand dollar life insurance policy on Mr. Layne."

Lusk stared at Torres, apparently trying to digest the words coming from her mouth. Eventually, he picked up the sheet of paper and studied it, his face blank. When he laid it back down, she continued.

"We examined robbery as a possible motive, and we did find an empty bank bag in the shop's office. However, through interviewing Detective Layne and visiting the bank, we determined there was little or no cash at the shop. Also, the victim's wallet contained forty dollars that wasn't taken."

"Okay. What about the murder weapon?"

Torres slid a copy of the ballistics report over to Lusk.

"The victim was shot twice with a 9 millimeter. We recovered an empty shell casing at the scene, plus the slugs from the victim. Detective Layne's service revolver is a 9 millimeter, and it was tested. It was not a match."

Lusk raised an eyebrow. "Then you can't put the gun in Detective Layne's hands?"

"Well, that would be true except for some information provided by the detective herself. She acknowledges purchasing a 9 millimeter handgun for her husband to keep at the shop. That gun is missing. As far as we can determine, she was the only one aware of its existence, and it has since disappeared."

So far, everyone else in the room had stayed silent, appearing much like observers at a tennis match, their heads rotating from Torres to Lusk and back again. As the latest volley settled on the district attorney, Lusk leaned back in his chair.

"Okay, now tell me about the exception to the timeline."

Torres pointed at the board. "Vanessa claimed to have returned after 12:15, found the body, then called 9-1-1 around 12:30. However, a 9-1-1 call was registered from the shop at 12:18 but was disconnected before it was answered."

"Did Detective Layne acknowledge making the call?"

"No. She never mentioned it. In addition, the neighborhood canvas turned up a witness. The owner of a screen printing shop across the street said he saw a yellow car speeding away from the garage at midnight."

"Yellow car?"

"Detective Layne drives a restored yellow Challenger."

Lusk studied the timeline. "So if she leaves when she says she does, she's not there to commit the murder. However, if she's there at midnight as the witness said, it puts Detective Layne at the shop at the time of the shooting."

Torres nodded. "Yes."

"Did the witness hear any gunshots?"

"Unfortunately, the witness was wearing headphones at the time."

Lusk closed his eyes, listening and thinking. "Did he see any other vehicles visit the garage?"

"No. Just the yellow car belonging to Detective Layne."

"So who do you think made the first 9-1-1 call?"

"I believe she returned to the shop earlier than 12:30, and made the call."

"And she hung up because?"

"Possibly to remove the weapon, tamper with evidence, or work on her story."

"What about prints? Did we find any on the phone?"

Torres shook her head. "The phone had been smeared with paint and revealed only a few partials, which were unusable. The rest of the prints found are still being processed."

Lusk sighed and stood. "Okay. Let's take ten, then Jason can tell me why I *shouldn't* have Detective Layne arrested."

Jason's throat tightened.

Lusk looked down at him. "No pressure, Detective."

****

When they returned to the room, Torres now sat where Jason had been before the break, and he stood by the board. When everyone had settled in, District Attorney Lusk cleared his throat.

"Jason, I know the case is circumstantial; heck, a first-year law student would know that. What I want from you is holes. Show me anything you have that pokes a hole in the theory put forward by Detective Torres."

"Yes, sir. First, let me say that a defense attorney is going to have a long line of people who support her character. You'll have to overcome a genuine sense of *she's not capable of doing it.* I would be on that list."

Lusk peered at him through eyes that were mere slits. "Detective Strong, isn't your former partner currently on paid suspension for losing her temper and striking a cuffed prisoner?"

Jason swallowed so hard he thought his Adam's apple would rupture. "Yes, but—"

Lusk held up a hand. "Just the facts, Detective, please."

"Yes, sir."

Jason turned to the board and pointed first at the firing range timeframe.

"It's well known that Detective Layne goes to the practice range regularly. It is not uncommon for her to go there at least once a week. If she were trying to cover up GSR evidence, she would have dressed appropriately to commit the crime. Gloves and a jacket could have prevented the suspicion that her time at the range suggests."

He pointed to the phone call noted between Vanessa and her sister. "The request to have her son stay with Miss Underwood is not unusual. When Vanessa was working, she would often have Kasen stay with her sister."

Lusk shrugged. "She's not working. Why leave him with the sister? If she wanted time with her husband, as she claimed, then she could put the boy to bed."

Jason considered arguing the point but decided against it. "Now, about the missing gun. It was purchased as a gift two years ago. It may have disappeared any time since then."

Lusk turned to Torres. "Have you found anyone who might have seen the gun recently?"

"No, sir. We have a list of Mr. Layne's customers, but it is extensive and we haven't had a chance to contact them all."

Lusk made a note, the first one since Jason started. He pressed on.

"The 9-1-1 call that logged at 12:18 could have been made by someone other than Detective Layne."

"Who?"

"I don't know. The killer, remorseful for what had happened, perhaps."

Lusk shook his head. "That still describes Detective Layne."

"But it could have been someone else."

"Okay. Let's say it was someone else who discovered the body while Layne was ditching the gun. Maybe they didn't want to get involved, but that still leaves Detective Layne as your killer."

Jason fought to conceal his frustration, both with the facts but especially at his inability to undermine the narrative given by Torres. He searched his memory for anything that contradicted the circumstantial case but found himself wondering if maybe, he just might be wrong.

Lusk seemed to sense Jason was stuck.

"Okay, look. Here's the case in a nutshell, as I see it. You all know it comes down to three things: motive, means, and opportunity. Motive depends on which item you think was the catalyst. The insurance would be pre-meditated murder. The fight about infidelity would be second-degree. Either way, there's a solid motive for the crime."

He crossed his arms and leaned back in the chair, coming perilously close to tipping backward yet managing to balance himself.

"Opportunity is also solid. She was there by her own admission, seen by a witness, and is placed on site by evidence such as the damaged phone. Whether it was just before midnight or just after, she is seen at the garage very close to the TOD."

He paused, and Jason wondered if it was on purpose, a Perry Mason moment for dramatic effect. Apparently, it wasn't. Lusk really seemed to be struggling with whether Vanessa had means or not.

"Detective Layne has the access to a 9 millimeter gun, even if it isn't her own, but that's not the issue. Without the murder weapon, we can't put it in her hands, and that can be reasonable doubt. However, it is likely she left the scene to dump the gun, probably somewhere we'll never find it."

Jason, who was still standing by the board, experienced a wave of despair flood over him. Lusk had just declared his opinion without stating his intentions. *He thinks she's guilty.*

The prosecutor rubbed his face with both hands.

"The thing that really sticks with me is the one fact you can't ignore in a circumstantial case. There are no alternative suspects. Nobody but Detective Layne is being looked at for the murder, and she meets the requirements to prosecute."

Danny Lusk sucked in a deep breath and stood, towering over the people sitting next to him. "Detectives, I appreciate your work and your candor. Please give your summations to Lieutenant Savage tonight, and, Eric, please have them on my desk by morning. Captain Morris, I expect to make a decision by tomorrow afternoon and will advise you then."

Without waiting for anyone to respond, he took two long strides to the door and was gone. Jason literally fell into a chair, his legs giving out. No one said a word for nearly five minutes, until finally, Captain Morris pushed on the table to, forcing herself to her feet.

"Jason, Dianna…I know this was very difficult for both of you. You both did a fine job under trying circumstances."

She looked at Savage. "I'll be in my office if you need me."

SHADOW OF DOUBT

He nodded, and Morris left.

Moments later, the lieutenant got up and moved to the door. He paused and looked back at Jason and Torres. "You both have reports to write. Get them done, and call it a day."

He closed the door behind him as he left. Torres shifted uncomfortably in her chair, but her eyes remained focused on Jason. Aware she was staring at him, he avoided meeting her gaze.

They sat in silence for a long time, neither making a move to leave. Eventually, Dianna leaned forward on the table, lowering her chin until it almost touched the surface. She stared up at him, attempting to make eye contact.

"Jason, I don't *want* it to be true. I was just doing my job."

He nodded but couldn't speak.

She sighed. "Look, there's still a possibility Lusk will refuse to indict. It's far from a slam dunk."

She was right, but that wasn't what had him so down. She couldn't know, but her narrative had impacted on his conviction. Somehow, she had enabled him to consider the possibility that Vanessa *could* have done it.

Torres stood. "I'm sorry."

Jason finally looked up. "Don't be."

John C. Dalglish

Chapter 12

Jason found himself sitting alone in the conference room, unsure what to do next. There were no leads to follow up and no suspects to interview. Seemingly, nothing he could say or do would stop the train that had already left the station. Inside, he knew an inconceivable truth.

Vanessa is going to be indicted for murder.

Saying it, even in his own mind, made it seem even more surreal. But like a bullet leaving the barrel of a gun, there was no stopping it. At least, not until it did its damage.

His phone vibrated, and he answered without looking to see who was calling. "Jason Strong."

"Come up to my office."

It took him a second to recognize the voice. "Yes, ma'am."

"Don't say where you're going."

SHADOW OF DOUBT

The line went dead. He double-checked the name to be sure he was right, then pushed himself up and out of the chair.

Out on the precinct floor, the door to the lieutenant's office was closed, and Torres was apparently off on some errand or another. He took the stairs up one floor.

Mary Faldo smiled warmly when she saw him. "Jason, nice to see you. How are you holding up?"

He returned her smile. "Let's just say I've had better days."

She nodded. "I'm sure of it. Go in. She's expecting you."

"Thanks, Mary."

He pushed the partially open door wide and went in to find Sarah Morris standing by the window, scanning the street below.

She didn't turn around. "Close the door, please."

Jason did.

"Pull up a seat, Jason."

He did that, too.

Choosing one of the hardback chairs in front of the captain's desk, he sat hunched forward, although he wasn't sure why. Perhaps he was preparing for the unexpected—steeling himself against an oncoming truck he couldn't see, bracing himself for an impact.

"Did you know that John Patton hated this job?"

She was still turned away, but he nodded anyway. "Yes. The politics, mostly, I believe."

"That was a big part of it, but there was something else."

"I guess I wasn't aware."

She slowly rotated in his direction, and he was surprised to see redness in her eyes. "He despised the fact that sometimes he had to make decisions that hurt the people he cared about."

"That sounds like John."

She stared at him, and he sensed she was stalling.

"What is it, Sarah?"

"It's…well…although Lusk said it would be tomorrow before he made his decision…"

Jason's breath stuck in his chest as he struggled with his words. "She's going to be… He's going to indict…her."

"Yes."

Blood pounded in his ears as he tried desperately to grasp the truth he'd accepted intellectually but had been unable to prepare for emotionally.

Morris moved around to her desk chair and dropped into it heavily.

"I have two things to ask you."

Jason was only half listening. "What are they?"

Apparently, the glazed look in his eyes gave him away. "Jason, focus. I need you with me."

Without realizing it, he'd fallen against the back of the chair, no longer leaning forward and attentive. He forced himself back into a sitting position. "I'm sorry. What do you need?"

"First, when the warrant is issued, do you want to deliver it?"

Jason tried to picture Vanessa in cuffs, being taken downtown in a black and white. There was no way he would allow that.

"Most definitely."

Sarah nodded. "I thought you'd say that, but that means you can't tip off Vanessa, or I'll have to use someone else."

"Okay. Is there any chance Lusk will change his mind?"

She shrugged. "I suppose, but that's not the impression I got."

It wasn't the impression Jason had gotten, either. "What's the other thing you wanted to talk about?"

She opened a notepad sitting on the desk. "You felt there were a couple things that weren't solid evidence. The missing gun and the second 9-1-1 call, among others."

Jason didn't remember the captain taking notes at the meeting, but obviously, she had been paying attention. "That's my opinion."

"I want you to spend the next several days trying to prove your point. Assuming she is booked tomorrow, Vanessa will have a preliminary hearing within a couple days. That hearing will be her best chance to get the case thrown out before going to trial."

He had been so wrapped up in his own emotions, it hadn't occurred to him to consider other folks' opinions. He cocked his head to one side. "You don't think she's guilty, either, do you?"

She stared at him, their eyes locked on each other's face. "No."

Jason was suddenly energized. "I thought I was the only one!"

She held up her hands as if to slow him down. "Look, officially, I'm not supposed to take a stand. Unofficially, I can't see Vanessa ever killing someone she loves."

"You and me both."

"So take a few days away from the precinct, follow your hunches, and see what you can come up with. Call me if you need anything from the department files that you can't access via your laptop."

Jason stood. "Thanks, Sarah."

"Don't thank me. You and I both know, despite our belief in Vanessa, that we could be dead wrong."
"Let's hope not."
"I am."

****

Jason headed out immediately after meeting with Sarah, partly because he wanted to avoid Torres and Savage but mostly because he needed to talk to Sandy. If he were going to find a way to clear Vanessa, he would have to get control of his emotions. Sandy was the one person who could help him accomplish that.

She was just starting dinner when he came through the door. "That you, Jason?"
"Yeah."

She came out of the kitchen. "You're home early. What's the occasion?"

He couldn't bring himself to smile at her joke. "Rough day."

Her smile disappeared as she came over and hugged him...the long hug, the one that said: *I'm glad you're home safe again, and I'm here for you.*

When she turned him loose, she took his hand and dragged him toward the kitchen. "Come on, I'll get us a glass of wine."

"It's a little early, isn't it? And don't say it's five o'clock somewhere!"

"Okay, I won't…but it is."

He groaned. "I hate that song."

"Save your complaints until after the first glass of wine."

Now he smiled, despite his mood. She had proven once again that she was just what he needed. While she poured the wine, he went and kissed the kids. When he returned to the kitchen with Penny in tow, the two of them sat and watched her cook dinner.

They ate together as a family and watched some TV afterward. Eventually, Sandy put the kids to bed. It wasn't until after she came back from tucking them in that she even asked.

"What's going on at the station?"

He set down his empty wineglass. "Morris advised me that Vanessa is likely to be arrested and charged with Rob's murder."

She sipped the last of her wine, keeping her feelings obscured behind the piece of stemware. "Likely?"

"My impression was almost certainly."

"Hmmm. Lusk?"

"Yeah. Apparently, there's enough evidence, to his way of thinking."

"Politics playing a part in it?"

He grunted. "Again, almost certainly."

"So what now?"

"Morris called me up to her office, making sure I didn't alert Torres or Savage."

"Oh?"

"She wanted to give me a heads-up and said she would let me be the one to bring Vanessa in."

"That was good of her."

"Yeah, but there was something else. She confided she didn't believe Vanessa could have done the murder. She wanted me to take a few days away from the precinct and work to prove it if I can."

Sandy appeared puzzled. "Isn't that what you've been doing?"

"Well, sure. But she suggested I focus on a couple points in particular and that I work alone."

"I assume you agreed."

"Of course."

"So I have a couple questions."

"Okay, shoot."

Her face darkened. "Are you prepared to be wrong?"

He'd known the question was coming and had asked himself multiple times. He gave her the same answer he'd given himself. "I guess I'll have no choice if it comes to that. Still, I can't quit on Vanessa."

"Of course you can't, and I would expect nothing less. Just know I'll be here if things turn out badly."

"I know, and I love you for it." He kissed her cheek. "Now what was your other question?"

"Will you get us another glass of wine?"

He kissed her again. "Your wish is my…well, you know how it goes."

She laughed. "I recorded *Jeopardy*. When you get back, I'll show you who the smart one in the family really is."

****

Since waking up just over an hour before, he'd sat in the kitchen, sipping coffee and waiting. Not because he was a pessimist, nor did he have a crystal ball, but only because he knew. On the inside, deep down, he knew.

Maybe it was the pale reality of morning, or it could just be that he'd resigned himself to her arrest. One thing it wasn't—it wasn't because he now believed her to be guilty.

He hadn't been staring at his phone when it began to ring, but he had been waiting.

"This is Strong."

"Jason, it's Sarah."

His breathing stopped, and all noise faded into the background; even his heart seemed to have ceased beating. When he didn't respond, she said it anyway.

"A warrant has been issued for the arrest of Vanessa Layne."

The formality of the statement struck him as odd, even ludicrous. It would have made more sense to say just that he needed to bring Vanessa in.

"Jason?"

His breathing restarted, and his heart resumed its rhythm, albeit pounding harder than he could ever remember. "Yeah?"

"Did you hear me?"

"Yes. I'll take care of it."

"Okay, but Lusk had a condition on you handling the arrest."

Jason didn't care what Lusk wanted. "What is his problem?"

"She has to be here by noon. If not, he'll send out a couple black and whites."

"Tell him to buzz off. I don't need his trust, and Vanessa won't create a soundbite for his political witch-hunt!"

"Jason?" She paused. "I'm on your side, remember?"

He made a physical attempt to control his emotions. "Sorry, Captain. That wasn't meant for you. We'll be there on time."

"I know. Bye."

The line went dead, and Jason found he was squeezing his phone so tight that his knuckles were white.

"Who was that?"

Startled, he dropped the phone. "I didn't see you there."

"Clearly. I gather that was about the warrant."

He nodded. "I have to bring her downtown before noon."

Sandy looked up at the clock. "You've got a little over three hours. You need to let her know, so she can prepare."

"I will. I just wanted a minute to think about what I was going to say."

Sandy's gaze was sympathetic as well as understanding. "I don't think you need to worry about it. She'll know as soon as she hears your voice."

She turned, going back to whatever it was she was doing and leaving him there staring at his phone.

****

SHADOW OF DOUBT

In the days since Rob's death, Vanessa had fallen into a predictable pattern. Mostly because it involved not having to think about what she was going to do next. In reality, it wasn't all that much different from what she had been doing every day since he'd moved into the shop.

She'd get up early, have coffee, then wake up Kasen. After getting his breakfast into him, she would get him dressed, and they would load up in the car. Twenty minutes later, she'd drop him off at pre-school.

That part of her day always involved avoiding eye contact with the other moms and dads dropping off their kids. She could see them staring, but no one said anything; not even the teachers would exchange the usual pleasantries with her. She blamed the articles in the San Antonio News for her status of pariah.

Returning home, she might try to do some laundry, maybe start the dishwasher. Nevertheless, it wasn't long before she was on the couch, staring at the photo album in her lap. Playing on the TV in the background would be *The Price is Right* or *Family Feud.*

Eventually, she'd wipe her eyes, check the time, and then force herself to get up.

After fixing her make-up, she'd pick up Kasen and go over to Rachel's place. Her sister was nothing less than a Godsend and managed to get Vanessa through each afternoon until it was time to go home and make dinner for Kasen.

This day was following the same pattern, and she had just turned on the TV when the phone rang.

"Hello?"

"Hey, Vanessa. It's me."

She paused, the tone in his voice constricting her throat. "Is there news?"

"I'm afraid so."

"Are you coming over?"

"I am. Should be there in about thirty minutes."

"Okay. I'll be ready."

She set down the phone and clicked off the TV. Opening the photo album, she extracted a family photo from Galveston Island and tucked it in her pocket.

SHADOW OF DOUBT

John C. Dalglish

Chapter 13

He pulled up in front of her house and put the car into park. He'd done the very same thing a thousand times, waiting for her to come out so they could work on a case; this visit was not like that. His mission to Vanessa's home was straight out of his worst nightmare.

He looked toward the house, wondering if she was watching and would come out ready to leave. Nothing stirred around the door or windows, and it suddenly became apparent the house was closed up tighter than usual. All the curtains were drawn, the house was dark, and even her car was gone.

His pulse surged. *She wouldn't!*

Suddenly pulled from his self-pitying reminiscence, he jumped from the car and ran to the front door. Knocking with more force than necessary, he found himself actually surprised when the door swung wide.

"Oh, you're here."

Her eyes, though red and swollen, widened briefly. "What did you think? That I'd gone on the run. From what?"

"Uh…well." His shoulders sagged. "I don't know what I thought. Nothing seems to make sense anymore. Your car was gone, so…"

"The car is in the garage, Jason. I figured I wouldn't need it for a while."

"Of course. Forgive me."

Her tone softened. "Nothing to forgive. We're all feeling a little displaced these days. Come in."

Jason followed her through the door and was troubled by how much her clothes hung on her. He wondered how much weight she'd lost. Wearing a red t-shirt, gray sweatpants, and white sandals, she looked as if they were heading to the beach or the gym.

"You know why I'm here, don't you?"

"I assumed it was to take me downtown for booking."

"It was that obvious?"

"We've been friends for a long time, Jason. Besides, I was told how the polygraph turned out."

He shrugged. "I told them they shouldn't be arresting you, but Lusk had other ideas."

"I kinda sensed it from the stories in the paper. I imagine they're under a lot of heat downtown."

"Sure, but that's no excuse to arrest an innocent person."

She smiled and reached a hand up to touch his face. "You're the best partner I could've ever hoped for."

He stared at her, touched by her words, but then grimaced as their meaning hit him. "Why are you talking in the past tense?"

"Oh, come on, Jason. Even if I beat this wrap, we both know my days at SAPD are over."

His frustration surfaced. "That's a bunch of crap! I don't ever want to hear that again, you understand?"

She didn't argue the point. Instead, she turned to a hall table and picked up a key. "This is to the house. Just in case you need to get in."

"What about Kasen?"

"Rachel is picking him up from pre-school, and he'll stay with her until this is over."

He accepted the key. "I'll give it to Sandy. You know me."

She managed to laugh. "Yes, I do. You'll lose it."

"Are you ready?"

The light moment vanished as quickly as it appeared. "I guess I have to be."

"I'm sorry I have to do this."

They stepped out into the morning sun's warmth, and she locked the door then turned to look at him. "I'm just glad it's you."

As they reached his car, she went to sit in the back. Jason quickly opened the front passenger door. "Up here will be fine."

She didn't argue and slid into the car. When he pulled the car away from the curb, he found he didn't know what to say. The situation was so far from anything he'd ever imagined, he didn't have a clue how to act. She seemed to be having the same difficulty.

The silence closed in on them, seemingly pulling the oxygen from the car, and Jason had to fight to keep it together. If he was this upset, he couldn't imagine what was going through Vanessa's mind. Her hands weren't trembling, and no tears appeared on her face.

She has that same calm demeanor she uses to study crime scenes.

That thought prompted a reminder.

"How long since you'd seen it?"

She looked at him, her eyebrows knitted in confusion. "Sorry?"

"The gun. The 9 millimeter you bought Rob. When was the last time you saw it?"

Her brows knitted together as she pondered the question. "Shoot… I can't remember. Four months ago, maybe six."

"Was it in the same place he always kept it?"

"Yeah. Why?"

"I started wondering if the gun may have been missing long before the night Rob was killed."

"You mean like it was stolen?"

"Or he sold it."

She shook her head. "Nah, I doubt it."

"What did it look like?"

"It was a Pro-9 with a chrome slide and thumb safety."

He glanced at her quickly. "Would he have told you if he sold it?"

She nodded. "I would assume so. It was a gift."

Jason sighed. "You're probably right."

The precinct came into view, and Vanessa visibly shrank into the seat. "This is the worst part."

"What is?"

"The booking. Every one of those people in there is…was my friend. What will they think?"

"Most will think exactly what I think. This is wrong. And those who don't feel that way aren't your friends to begin with."

Her lips trembled. "You're right."

"Do you have a lawyer?"

"Yeah. The same guy who was representing me in the disciplinary appeal. He's going to come by after I'm processed."

"Good. Call me or Sandy if you need anything, got it?"

"I will."

They pulled up at the door to booking. She stared at it then turned to Jason. "You'll come see me, won't you?"

His eyes welled up, and anger surged over him like a river of burning oil. He could feel his face reddening and sensed his breathing had become labored.

This is insane! They can't do this to her. They shouldn't do this to Kasen. Everything about this is wrong!

"Jason?"

He brushed at his eyes with the back of his hand. Trying but mostly failing, he attempted to gain control. "You can count on it."

She studied him for a moment, seeming to contemplate saying something more, but decided against it. He thought she appeared more worried about him than herself.

They climbed out of the car and entered Booking. There wasn't much for him to do then, so he just stayed close. When the photos, prints, and paperwork were done, she turned to him. Putting on a brave face, she smiled.

"Thanks, Jason."

Still struggling with his anger, he nodded stiffly. "You're welcome, but save the real gratitude for when I get you out."

"Okay." Her smile disappeared, and then she was gone, too.

He turned abruptly and stormed out of the precinct. He had work to do.

****

The Romanesque architecture of the Bexar County Courthouse gave it a look that mixed an inner-city high school with a Roman cathedral. Located just west of the Riverwalk, the red sandstone structure built in 1892 now served as the county seat. Therefore, the historic, four-story building was home to the office of District Attorney Danny Lusk.

Jason had calmed down considerably by the time he got there and was pleased to find Lusk was available. After getting the all clear from the receptionist, Jason found himself inside the ornate, wooden interior of the D.A.'s office. Dark wood, aged over many years, was counterbalanced by a large, arching window that let in plenty of light.

Lusk stood when Jason came in, and they shook hands.

"Jason! Good to see you. How did it go with Miss Layne?"

"No problem. I just came from there."

Lusk sat back down in the gold, overstuffed chair from which he'd risen. "I received word she was in custody."

Jason's anger attempted to resurface. *In custody* sounded as if Vanessa had been on the run and finally captured. He took a deep breath.

"What will it take to have the charges dropped?"

The redheaded prosecutor regarded him, a level of astonishment on his face. Lacing his fingers together, he stared at Jason for a long time.

"I'm not sure how to answer that. Are you here on behalf of her lawyer or as her friend?"

"Neither. I'm here as a San Antonio Homicide detective who believes we have the wrong person."

"I see."

"I want to know what evidence would convince *you* that you're prosecuting the wrong individual."

Lusk's demeanor remained impassive. "That assumes I agree with you and think it's possible to find such evidence."

"Frankly, I don't care whether you agree or not. I am interested only in why you went ahead with the prosecution, and what would stop it."

Lusk stared at him some more, and Jason began to wonder if he'd overstepped his bounds. In his anger, he hadn't considered whether it was appropriate for an SAPD officer to barge into the D.A.'s office. So just when Jason became convinced he would leave empty-handed, surprisingly, Lusk let out a long sigh.

"Okay. Look, we've worked together before, and I know you're a good cop. Here's what I'll give you, and this is it, you understand?"

Jason bobbed his head and waited.

"One of the biggest things that Detective Layne has to overcome is the lack of another suspect. There's no one else who could have or would have wanted to commit this murder. You know the old saying—if it walks like a duck…"

"So I need to find a credible alternative to Vanessa in order to cast doubt on her prosecution?"

"It would certainly help."

Jason stood. "Thank you, sir."

He headed for the door.

"Jason…"

"Sir?"

"Good luck."

****

Jason returned to his car. An alternative suspect was what he needed, but his first thought was he had to take the gun out of Vanessa's hand. If he could find Rob's handgun and prove it wasn't the murder weapon, he would worry about putting a different gun in someone else's hand later.

Vanessa believed Rob would have told her if he sold the gun, but things were not as they should have been between them. Jason felt it was possible Rob might have pawned the gun for cash, not bothering or wanting to tell her.

Opening his laptop, he typed in the address of Rob Layne's body shop. The Google map opened up, and on the menu, he clicked *nearby* link. In the search window, he punched in *pawn and gun shops.*

Three shops were listed: *Cash America, Pronto Pawn,* and *American Loan.*

Jason opened his phone and dialed the first on the list.

"Cash America. This is Sherry."

"Hi, Sherry. I'm looking for a particular handgun. Can you help me?"

"I'll try."

"It's a Browning 9 millimeter, the model Pro-9. Any chance you guys have that model in your inventory?"

"Let me get over by the case we keep those in."

Jason listened to background noise as the clerk moved around the store. After less than a minute, she came back on the line. "We have two."

Jason's pulse accelerated. "Do either of them have a chrome slide?"

"No. Both are matte black."

"That's too bad. I'm after one with the chrome slide. Thanks for your help."

"Any time."

Disappointed, Jason hung up then dialed the next shop.

"Pronto Pawn."

"Hi. Who's this?"

"Manny."

"Manny, I'm looking for a particular handgun."

"Okay, shoot!"

Jason forced a tiny laugh, more to be polite than because the joke was funny. "It's a Browning Pro-9."

"Oh, yeah. Those are nice guns. Usually, I sell them as quick as I get 'em."

"Do you have any at the moment?"

"Just one."

Jason cautioned himself about getting his hopes up. "Is it the model with the chrome slide and safety?"

"As a matter of fact, yes."

Jason took a quick look at the shop's address. "I'm very interested in it. I'll be there in ten minutes."

"Great. See you then."

Jason snapped his phone shut and started the car. *Pronto Pawn* was the closest shop to Rob's garage, making it the most likely one he would use. Adrenaline pushed him to drive a little faster than he should have.

Seven minutes later, he arrived outside the pawn and gun store. Complete with large signage and a blow-up manikin bobbing back and forth in the wind, the orange-and-white concrete structure stood out not for what it had but for what it lacked—

windows. Not one on the entire building, not even in the door.

When he first entered, it took his eyes a moment to adjust to the darkness inside. Once they had, he found a well-organized and clean store. Shelves had rows of power tools with bright-green price stickers, guitars hung on a rack with similar tags dangling from the strings, and guns filled the glass cabinets at the front.

The young man at the counter sported a blue, button-down shirt with *Pronto Pawn* emblazoned across the pocket. The nametag on the opposite side of his chest read Manny. In his late twenties or early thirties, Manny had the sculpted muscles of a body builder. He looked up from cleaning one of the glass gun cabinets. "Afternoon. Can I help you?"

Jason pulled out his badge and held it up for inspection. "I'm Detective Strong with SAPD Homicide. I called you a few minutes ago about the Pro-9."

Manny blanched slightly. "Yeah, sure. It's over here."

Jason matched steps with Manny, he on the outside of the gun cases and Manny on the inside. When Manny reached the corner cabinet, he unlocked the back of the case and slid the door open. He bent over and seconds later stood up, holding a gun that looked exactly as Vanessa had described it. The odds were extremely long that this was the same weapon, but Jason was feeling lucky.

Manny handed him the gun, and Jason turned it over in his hands as if it was a newborn baby. "Do you have the records on this?"

Manny lifted the paper tag attached to the trigger guard and looked at the number. Reaching behind him, he pulled out a spiral-bound notebook and laid it on the counter. After running his finger down several pages, he finally stopped over a name.

"Here it is. We purchased the gun two weeks ago from a Robert Layne."

Jason stared at the man's mouth, not certain he'd heard him correctly. "Did you say Layne?"

"Yeah."

"What address did he give?"

"811 Broadway."

Jason looked down at the gun. For the first time since the murder, something had gone their way. There was no doubt that when this gun was tested, it would not be a match for the murder weapon.

He had taken *this* gun out of Vanessa's hand, but that didn't mean she couldn't have used a different weapon, at least as far as Lusk was concerned.

What he needed now was to put a gun in someone else's hand—and not just any gun but the murder weapon.

SHADOW OF DOUBT

Chapter 14

After securing a warrant from Sarah Morris to confiscate the gun and delivering the Pro-9 to Doc Josie, he went up to his desk.

"Hey, Jason."

Though he'd hoped to avoid talking to anyone, Torres was sitting at her desk.

"Hey."

"I was told you were going to take a few days off."

"Yeah, sort of. I need to tie up some loose ends on stuff."

"Anything I can help with?"

"No, but thanks."

The phone on her desk rang, and when she answered, Jason took the opportunity to grab what he'd come for and leave. Torres was just hanging up as he got on the elevator. He waved as the door closed, even though she seemed to be getting up to follow him.

He didn't hold the door.

Twenty minutes later, he'd secured a booth at the back of a nearby Denny's restaurant.

"What can I get ya', hon'?"

"Coffee, black."

"Anything to eat?"

"Not right now, thanks."

"Be right back."

Jason opened the file marked *Neighborhood Canvas—Case #17453—Layne.*

Reading at a deliberate and careful pace, he began to work his way through the pile of interviews, literally line by line.

His coffee arrived in a thermal carafe. He finished it, had it re-filled, and was well into the next pot when he got to the report taken from the screen printer. Purposely keeping it to study last, Jason emptied the final drops of coffee into his cup. The single most damning evidence against Vanessa was in this interview because it discredited her timeline.

He read it over twice, unable to find anything that struck him as inconsistent.

"More coffee?"

He rubbed his eyes. "No, thank you. I think I'll get out of your hair now."

"You're not botherin' me, hon'. Look around; this place is dead."

Jason smiled. "Nevertheless, I need to go see someone. Thanks again."

****

Fast and Fabulous screen-printing was a small establishment that sat diagonally across from Rob Layne's body shop. The heat had returned to South Texas, and like the night of the murder, the print shop's overhead garage door was up. When Jason parked, he observed a man in his mid-fifties sitting at a machine, doing the same function repeatedly.

He'd slide a piece of large paper over a table filled with holes; the paper would then be sucked flat by a vacuum. When the man removed his hands, the machine lowered a screen over the paper and pressed ink onto the sheet. The screen would lift, and a robotic arm would grab the paper.

The inked sheet was dropped onto a conveyer that ran toward a dryer oven, and the man would slide on the next piece of paper, starting the whole process again. It struck Jason as mind-numbing work, but the man seemed to be enjoying himself. That's when Jason noticed the man was wearing ear-buds. As he got out of the car, the man finally noticed Jason and smiled. At the end of one of the cycles, he punched a button to stop the press.

"Hola."

Jason produced his badge. "Good afternoon. I'm sorry to interrupt your work."

"No trouble. I need to add some ink, anyway."

"Are you Renaldo Garza?"

"Si."

"I'd like to ask you a few questions about what happened across the street the other night."

The round man with wide-set eyes smiled easily, and despite the heat, he didn't appear to be bothered by the warmth or having to answer questions.

"I told the cops everything that night, but I'm glad to repeat it for you."

"I appreciate it."

"Do you mind if I add some ink while we talk?"

"Not at all. Would you go over the events of that night for me?"

Renaldo picked up a gallon can that sat next to the press and poured a generous portion onto the screen.

"Well, let's see. I was sitting right here, finishing up an order, when I saw the yellow car speed away."

"Could you see the driver?"

"Not well. I think it was a woman."

"What time was that?"

"Very close to midnight."

Any optimism Jason had arrived with was quickly evaporating. He looked around for a clock on the shop walls. "I don't see a clock. How did you know what time it was?"

"The only clock is in the office. I knew the time because I was listening to the Astros play the Yankees. The announcer had said it was almost midnight when the game went into the final inning. It couldn't have been more than twenty or thirty minutes later when I saw the car."

"What about other activity? Are you sure you didn't notice anyone else around that night?"

Garza shook his head slowly. "No, it was quiet. After most folks went home, I was one of the few still open along the street. The only thing I saw was a traffic stop done at the end of the block."

Jason's ears perked up. "Traffic stop?"

"Yeah, but it was earlier."

"How much earlier?"

"Oh, I don't know. An hour, maybe ninety minutes."

Jason took out his pad and made a note. "Did you see the vehicle?"

"Nah. I wasn't too interested."

"Was there anything else?"

Garza shook his head. "No."

Jason shook the man's hand. "Thank you for your time."

"De nada."

Jason got back in the car and checked the time. It had been a long day, and emotionally, he was spent. He called Sandy.

"Hello?"

Her voice immediately raised his spirits. "Hey, it's me."

"You headed home?"

"I am."

****

That night, after dinner with the kids and getting them off to bed, Jason poured himself and Sandy each a glass of wine. Penny laid at their feet as they snuggled on the couch. Enjoying his wife's company, sipping the wine in the quiet of the night, he reflected on how blessed he was. Rob and Vanessa could never have this kind of time together again.

He ran the events of the day over in his mind. It had started so badly but ended better than he'd hoped. The phone broke the silence, and Sandy reached it first.

"Hello?"

She looked a Jason and handed him the phone without comment.

"This is Jason."

"Jason, it's Doc Josie."

"Hey, Doc. You're not still working, are you?"

"I was just getting ready to head home, but I thought you might like to know I'd finished the testing on the gun."

"And?"

"As I'm sure you suspected…it was not a match. That gun was not the murder weapon."

"Great. Thanks, Doc."

He hung up and looked at Sandy, who was watching him intently. "That sounded like good news."

"It was. In a stroke of luck, I was able to locate the gun owned by Rob Layne."

"That's the one Lusk thinks Vanessa used to kill Rob, isn't it?"

"Yes. It wasn't the murder weapon."

She smiled broadly. "That's great news!"

"Yes, but it only goes so far."

Her smile tempered slightly. "What do you mean?"

"Lusk will claim she used a different weapon. It's a less-convincing theory than the missing gun but still reasonable. I have to put the gun that killed Rob in someone else's hand."

"Can you do that?"

He shrugged. "I'm gonna try, but without the gun it's hard to prove who used it."

They fell silent for a few minutes, but he sensed something was on his wife's mind.

He touched her hand. "What is it?"

"Oh…I just wondered how the arrest went."

Jason exhaled wearily. "Better than I expected, I guess. Although, after all the time I've known her, you wouldn't think anything Vanessa does could surprise me. Turns out, that's not true. She was composed, and in many ways handled it better than I did."

A sad smile curled her lips. "That sounds like the Vanessa I know."

Suddenly exhausted, he wanted only to sleep. He put his wineglass down and lay in her lap. She stroked his hair. Once, twice… If she did it a third time, he never felt her touch.

****

John C. Dalglish

Jason awoke with a start, and pushing himself upright, it took him several moments before he finally figured out he was still on the couch. A fuzzy memory of Sandy stroking his hair helped put the rest of the puzzle together. Still early, no one was awake except Penny. He let her out into the yard and went to have a shower. When he was ready to leave, everyone was still asleep, so he kissed Sandy goodbye and headed out.

Picking up the newspaper from the driveway, he resisted the urge to look at it before getting into the car. At a nearby Dunkin Donuts, he pulled in and went inside with the San Antonio News under his arm.

After ordering coffee and a donut, he unwrapped the paper. He wished he hadn't.

SAN ANTONIO PD DETECTIVE ARRESTED
Vanessa Layne charged with husband's murder

(Devin James, Major Crimes Reporter)

In what District Attorney Danny Lusk called a "strong case," a warrant was issued for the arrest of SAPD Detective

SHADOW OF DOUBT

Vanessa Layne. She was charged with the murder of her husband, Rob Layne, at his body shop last week.

Lusk said the warrant was executed, and Miss Layne was in custody. He also said no other individuals appear to have been involved. When asked what had convinced him to go ahead with the arrest of the respected detective, he declined to say.

Rob Layne was killed in his business by two gunshots to the chest. The gun suspected to be the murder weapon was owned by Rob Layne, but so far, it has not been recovered. Lusk said that finding the weapon was not imperative in taking the case to trial.

When asked if he would seek the death penalty, Lusk bristled. "At this time, the case does not seem to rise to the level of a death penalty case. However, we continue to evaluate all aspects of the crime."

Jason tossed the paper onto the counter. Rising to his feet, he prepared to leave.

"Mind if I look at your paper?"

Jason looked over at a gentleman sitting two chairs down. "Have at it. As far as I'm concerned, there's nothing good in it."

Chapter 15

Jason pulled into the parking lot at the precinct and shut off his car. Taking out his phone, he called Captain Morris.

"Captain Morris's office."

"Hi, Mary. It's Jason. Is the captain in?"

"Hey, Jason. Yeah, but she's on another line. Do you want to hold?"

"Sure."

Less than five minutes later, Sarah came on. "Morning, Jason."

"Morning, Sarah. Did you see the paper?"

"Yeah. Doesn't seem to be much we can do about it. The situation is what it is."

"Did you hear about the gun?"

"I did. Good work."

"It's a start."

"Hold on." She covered the phone then came back a few seconds later. "I've got to go. Was there something you needed?"

SHADOW OF DOUBT

"Yes. A witness reported a traffic stop on Broadway on the night Rob was killed. Can you get a copy of the dispatch logs for that night?"

"Sure. Email them to you?"

"Perfect."

"I'll do it. Gotta run."

Jason hung up and climbed out of the car. He was about to do something he never could have imagined…something he couldn't have prepared for. Visit his partner in jail.

Then again, strange things seemed to be happening a lot lately.

****

Rather than talking to her in her cell, Jason asked a guard to bring Vanessa to an interview room. While he waited, he found himself pacing the floor.

What's the matter with me? It's my partner. It's Vanessa.

He pulled out one of the chairs and sat down. Just then, the door opened. Jason jumped back to his feet.

Vanessa, now clothed in the traditional, orange, prison jumpsuit, fashioned a grin. "Nice of you to stand for a lady."

He grinned, suddenly self-conscious in front of her. "How are you making out in there?"

She shrugged and dropped into the chair opposite his. "Okay, I guess. They're keeping me by myself. Mostly, it's extremely boring."

"I can imagine…I mean…I bet it is."

She tipped her head to one side and studied him. "Jason, what's up with you?"

Jason found himself feeling sheepish. "I don't know. I guess I'm a little on edge. Everything is so screwed up."

"Well, cut it out! You're making me tense."

He laughed. "I'm sorry. Anyway, I do bring good news."

"Do tell."

"I found Rob's gun."

"Where?"

"A pawn shop near the garage. He sold it about two weeks ago."

Her eyes showed a spark for the first time. "That's great. Did you have it tested?"

"Yes. No match."

"So, whoever killed Rob didn't use his gun against him."

"Right."

Her shoulders sagged slightly. "But that won't get me out of here."

He reached across the table and touched her hand. "Hey, I'm still working on that."

She patted the top of his hand. "I know you are, and I appreciate it more than you can imagine."

"I won't let up."

"Speaking of not letting up. Did you see Devin's article in the paper today?"

Jason sat back in his chair, disgust radiating from his tone. "I don't get it. Why does he hate you so much? The guy has been merciless."

"Yeah. My lawyer's worried Devin is making it hard for me to find a fair jury."

"Is he considering asking for a change of venue?"

"If we get to that point, possibly."

Jason crossed his arms and stared at her. "You never told me what happened."

"With what?"

"With James. You two have disliked each other since before the Norman Lasiter case."

She averted her eyes. "It wasn't a big deal, at least not to me. When I applied for the position of homicide detective, my main competition was a department information officer."

"Who was that?"

"Bobby James."

Jason shrugged. "Doesn't ring a bell."

"Bobby was Devin's son."

Jason's mouth hung open. "James has a son?"

"Yeah. I guess you didn't know?"

"Not a clue."

"Anyway, my union rep argued that the department needed more female detectives, and John Patton agreed. That made the difference in me getting the position over Bobby."

"Why didn't you ever tell me this?"

She shrugged. "Didn't want you to think I *only* got the job because I was a female."

"You know me better than that. I might have joked about it, but your abilities are unquestionable."

"Thanks. Anyway, I guess, after a while, it just became water under the bridge."

"Apparently, not for Devin. He's sticking it to you."

"Yeah. I guess some people can't let things go."

Jason's phone buzzed. The captain had sent over the dispatch reports.

"I better get back to work."

"Of course. I do need a favor, though."

He smiled. "Anything."

"Will you go by the funeral home and pick up Rob's ashes?"

Jason's breath caught in his throat. "Uh...sure. You know I will. What do you want me to do with them?"

"You have my house key, right?"

"Sandy does."

"Just put them in the house for now."

"Consider it done."

Her smile was appreciative but forlorn. "Thanks."

She got up from the table and knocked at the door. A jailer came and escorted her out of the room. Jason sat, staring at the doorway through which she'd just vacated.

You're right about one thing, Strong. Everything is screwed up.

****

Jason had gone back out to his car and opened his laptop. While the dispatch logs were downloading, he pulled up *Google* search and typed in *MLB box scores*.

Something about his interview with Renaldo Garza was nagging at him. The timeline provided by the screen printer was critical to Vanessa's guilt or innocence, yet

Garza's only frame of reference for the time was a ballgame on the radio.

The search popped up several results, but he opted for the *Yahoo!* Sports link. Going back to the day of the murder, he found the Astros/Yankees game, or rather, two games. The teams had played a double-header.

Jason ran his finger down to the bottom of the information. Time of the first game was two hours and forty minutes. It began at 5:08 eastern time. He made a note and added the game time. Game one ended at 7:48 eastern time.

He dropped down and checked game two. The running time of it was three hours and fifty minutes. It began at 8:20 eastern time and went into extra innings. That put the end of game two at 12:10 a.m. eastern time.

Jason pulled out his notes on the interview with Garza and reread the quote referring to the timeline.

"I knew the time because I was listening to the Astros play the Yankees. The announcer had said it was almost midnight when the game went into the final inning. It couldn't have been more than twenty or thirty minutes later when I saw the car."

SHADOW OF DOUBT

The announcer had referred to midnight eastern *time. The time in San Antonio would have been 11:00 p.m., not midnight!*

His heart pounding in his ears, he came to the realization that the car speeding away at 12:30 was Vanessa's, but it was actually 11:30, just as she'd said.

When she returned at 12:30, Garza was already gone!

He picked up the phone to call the captain but it rang first.

"This is Strong."

"Jason, it's Sarah."

"Yes, ma'am. What's up?"

"Are you near the station?"

He looked through the windshield at the precinct. "As a matter of fact, yes."

"I need you to come up to my office."

"Now?"

"Yes, please."

"Very well. Be there shortly."

****

A mute and sullen Mary Faldo signaled him into the office. Once inside, he was surprised to discover a meeting going on. Sitting or standing in various spots about the room were Doc Davis, Lieutenant Savage, Doc Josie, and Dianna Torres.

Sitting behind her desk was Captain Morris. "Hi, Jason. Thanks for coming so quickly."

"Of course."

Walking gingerly, as if he needed to be careful or he might step on a grenade; he got over by the window and leaned against the wall. The lack of eye contact from his peers put him on edge.

Morris held up a copy of the morning's San Antonio News. "I assume all of you have read this."

Heads nodded all around.

"There is a detail in this story that was kept strictly under wraps. Those of you in this room were the only ones privy to the following: *Rob Layne was killed in his business by two gunshots to the chest.*"

She let the paper drop onto the desk. "What I want to know is who leaked the information to Devin James?"

She moved her gaze from person to person, pausing at each individual to make eye contact. No one flinched.

"Come on, people. Somebody released a critical investigative detail that might have solved this case, and I want to know who!"

The old saying about being able to "cut the tension with a knife" was nowhere near descriptive enough for the atmosphere in that room. Maybe an ax.

Jason had to force himself to breathe.

After several minutes of silence, Morris picked up the paper and tossed it into the trash.

"Okay. Since we have a leak but don't have a confession, then the following is now policy for the department. No one is to speak with Devin James. Not under any circumstances, or for any reason, unless authorized by me. Is that clear?"

More silently nodding heads.

"And to emphasize the importance of this, I want it known that anyone violating this policy will be immediately suspended without pay. Is that also clear?"

Head nodding was becoming rampant.

"Josie and Leonard, you pass it on to your people. Eric, you are to speak with your other detectives."

Sarah Morris glared around the room. "Any questions?"

Apparently, nobody was dumb enough to pose one.

"Good. Everyone out except Jason."

While the rest of the gang made their getaway, Jason was left trying to remember if he had ever seen the captain so angry. As the room emptied, he decided he hadn't.

Sarah went behind her desk. "Close the door, Jason."

He did then took a seat opposite her. "It wasn't me, I swear."

She waved her hand in dismissal. "I didn't keep you for that. I want an update on your work."

He explained what he'd learned about the timeline.

"Excellent work. I'm going to make Danny Lusk aware. Maybe that will be enough to delay his arraignment of Vanessa."

"When is that?"

"Tomorrow afternoon. Her lawyer will ask for a dismissal, but unless Lusk is on board, the judge won't grant it. "What's next on your agenda?"

"I haven't had a chance to go over the dispatch logs yet. I'm planning to spend some time on that this afternoon."

She nodded. "Very good. Now, the chief is waiting for a call, so excuse me."

Jason didn't need to be asked twice.

SHADOW OF DOUBT

John C. Dalglish

Chapter 16

When a detective is stuck and his case is going nowhere, dispatch logs can be invaluable. Sorting them by area, officer, or type of call can allow an investigator to get a feel for what was going on in proximity to his crime scene. The logs include any call from a car to dispatch and any response issued by the dispatcher.

Jason had printed out the email sent to him by the captain and found she had done some of the refining for him. The logs included only calls from the general area of downtown where Rob Layne's body shop was located.

He spread the sheets out on his desk.

Torres had gone off on another case, and Savage had locked himself in his office, which meant Jason should have an uninterrupted opportunity to study the logs.

Ten codes made up the bulk of the dispatch traffic, so he started by eliminating the routine ones. 10-24—assignment completed; 10-34—correct time requested; and 10-42—going off duty. These filled the logs but were of little use to him. The remainder pertained mostly to officer interactions with the public.

Of particular interest to him were the 10-38 calls—the code for a traffic stop. Jason found five of them between 8:00 and midnight on the evening Rob was killed. Two were speeding tickets, two were suspicion of drunk driving, and one was a burned out brake light. None took place on Broadway, and none was close to the time indicated by Garza.

"Dang it!"

He leaned back in his chair, stared at the logs, and wished he had heat ray vision. He'd torch the pile just out of aggravation. Closing his eyes, he pushed himself to come up with his next move.

What am I missing? Where do I go now?

He drew in a deep breath and exhaled loudly.

"You sound as if you're having a day like mine."

Jason opened his eyes to find Torres had returned. He rocked forward in his chair. "If you're frustrated, aggravated, and a bit pissed off, then yes, I am."

She smiled. "Sounds about right. What are those?"

"Dispatch logs." He gathered them up. "I was just about to toss them into…"

He stopped, his mind going over the ten codes.

10-92? Suspicious activity.

He checked the time of the call—10:45. Then he checked the location. 9th and Broadway.

That would be what Garza saw and assumed was a traffic stop.

His adrenaline pumping, he grabbed his laptop and punched in a request for the officer's notes from the stop. A brief narrative popped up on the screen.

Observed a lone individual sitting in a car, the engine not running and no lights on. The business he was parked in front of was closed. When questioned, the man reported he was waiting for a friend. I ran the plate and the man's license but found no reason to detain.

Jason scanned down to see the name of the driver.

"You're joking!"

Torres was watching him. "What?"

SHADOW OF DOUBT

He looked up, surprised by his outburst. "That slime ball was in the area the night of Rob Layne's murder."

"Which slime ball?"

"Devin James!"

"Didn't you say he was the first member of the press to show up?"

"That's right. No one else had even sniffed out the story yet."

"I guess it helps to be lucky."

Jason wasn't buying it. "Yeah, or have advance notice of what was going down."

Torres looked incredulous. "Oh, come on. The killer gave him a heads-up, and James didn't report it? I can't buy that for a minute."

"I guess it does sound ridiculous."

Jason rubbed his temples, letting ideas bounce around his thoughts.

Still, it's too much of a coincidence, and I don't like coincidences.

He grabbed a piece of paper and scribbled down what he knew about James that was related to the case.

In area.
First on scene.
Feud with Vanessa
Knew about the two gunshots.

He looked up at Torres, who was now regarding him with a mix of skepticism and concern.

"The two gunshots! Devin wrote about the two shots to the chest, but no one copped to telling him."

She didn't lose her skeptical look but he could see her mind working.

Suddenly, she opened up her computer, punched in some information, hit enter, and waited. Jason could tell when the information she sought had popped up; the blood drained from her face.

"Devin James has a registered gun."

"Let me guess. A 9 millimeter."

Her jaw seemed to have locked but she managed to nod.

Jason stood and headed toward the stairs. "I'm going to talk with Morris."

****

Mary Faldo looked a little less tense when he arrived to see the captain. "Is she in, Mary?"

"Yes, but the D.A. is with her."

"Lusk?"

"Yes."

"Perfect. Tell them I'm here, will you?"

Mary picked up the phone, and a moment later, nodded at Jason. He went to the door, knocked, and entered. Lusk and

Morris were sitting in a couple of armchairs discussing something. Sarah waved Jason to an open chair, but he opted to stand.

"Captain, I need a warrant."

If she was surprised, she hid it. "Why didn't you ask Lieutenant Savage?"

"This warrant request has special circumstances attached to it."

"Okay… What's it for?"

"A gun."

She sighed, obviously irritated with the guessing game. "Whose gun, Jason?"

"Devin James."

She stared at him, her surprise evident. Danny Lusk turned to look at Jason. "Did you say James?"

"Yes, sir."

"Isn't that the reporter who has been frying our butts in the press?"

"The same."

Lusk's face reddened significantly. "Have you lost your mind? Why in the world would you poke that bear?"

Jason stood his ground. "You remember telling me to find another suspect? Devin James is that person."

"Based on what?"

"I can put him in the area of the crime that night. He has an ongoing feud with Detective Layne, and he was on scene before anyone else in the press even knew about the killing."

"Pfft! You're going to need a whole lot more than that."

Jason turned to Sarah. "Our discussion of who leaked the information about two shots?"

She nodded.

"What if it was never leaked? What if he knew all along?"

"The only way he could know that would be…"

Jason nodded. "If he was the shooter."

His superiors exchanged looks, and the atmosphere in the room became electric. Sarah stood and went behind her desk but didn't sit down.

"The gun? Is it a 9?"

"Yes, ma'am."

She started to write out the warrant request. Lusk was rubbing his chin, probably trying to digest what Jason had just said. "The feud? What's that about?"

"Devin James has a son who is with the SAPD. He was up for detective at the same time as Vanessa, and the job went to Layne. I've witnessed strife between the two ever since but didn't know why."

Lusk was shaking his head. "That's mighty thin! In fact, almost invisible."

SHADOW OF DOUBT

Sarah finished the warrant and handed it to Jason then looked at Lusk. "I've seen people kill for less. Jason, get the gun."

"Yes, ma'am."

****

Devin James lived in a condo on the north side of the city. It bordered a golf course, but Jason had never seen the reporter with a golf club in his hand. Torres followed Jason as they climbed the steps to the second-story unit and knocked.

A moment later, the door opened. "Jason! What brings you out here?"

He handed the warrant to James. "This does. I'm here to take possession of a firearm you own."

James stared at the warrant. "The 9 millimeter? I haven't had that gun for ages."

"Oh? What happened to it?"

"It was stolen."

"Oh? Did you file a police report?"

Devin handed the warrant back. "No. I just figured it was gone for good."

The reporter was selling, but Jason wasn't buying. "Step aside, Devin. The warrant gives us the right to search the condo and your office."

"I want to call my attorney."

Jason grinned at him. "I don't care if you call your momma. The search is happening right now."

Both Torres and Jason pushed past Devin and began systematically going through the apartment. They looked in every drawer, under every couch cushion, and pulled out all of his clothes. Jason's frustration grew as James sat and watched.

"I told you. It was stolen."

Jason ignored him. Torres came out of the bedroom. "What now?"

"Did you check under the mattress?"

She turned and went back. Jason returned to the bathroom and rechecked everywhere. The cabinet held nothing, under the sink was just cleaners, and the shower was empty.

Torres stuck her head inside. "Nothing under the mattress."

Jason nodded then reached for the lid on the toilet tank. A smile crept across his face.

"What have we here?"

He reached inside and lifted out a Ziploc bag containing a gun. Jason nodded toward Devin. "Dianna, let's take Mr. James downtown for some questioning."

"Sounds like a plan."

SHADOW OF DOUBT

John C. Dalglish

Chapter 17

Jason stood in the observation room, arms crossed, looking through the glass at Devin James. For the last forty minutes, the reporter had alternated between sitting and pacing. The gun had been delivered to Doc Josie for testing, and Jason was stalling.

Next to him, Lieutenant Savage was on the phone.

"Good. Let me know as soon as you can." He closed his phone. "The fire test is done, and they're doing the comparison exam now."

Jason nodded. "Time to see if our boy is up to answering a few questions."

Moving to the interview room, Jason pushed open the door.

Devin, who was currently pacing, froze. "Finally! I've got things to do, you know."

"I guess they'll have to wait. You're not going anywhere for a while."

SHADOW OF DOUBT

Jason sat down and stared up at Devin. "Care to take a seat?"

"If it'll speed things along, gladly."

Jason waited until they were facing each other. "I think we both know what ballistics on your gun will show."

Devin stared at him but didn't answer.

"I can put you in the area both before and immediately after the murder. You have knowledge that was not public…"

"What knowledge?"

"Outside a small contingent of this department, you're the only one who knew Rob Layne had been shot twice, not just once. Even the onsite EMTs thought it was a single gunshot."

Devin rolled his eyes. "I had an inside source."

"Oh? I'll need a name."

"You know I won't reveal a source."

Jason shrugged. "Suit yourself, but a jury isn't going to give a crap about your ethics. They'll want proof."

"A jury? Am I being charged with something?"

"We'll get to that. First, I want to know why you lied about your gun."

The muscles in Devin's face twitched, and his lips tightened. Suddenly, eye contact was difficult for the reporter.

A knock at the door broke the silence.

Jason stood and opened it to find Savage motioning him into the hallway. Holding his breath, Jason stared at the lieutenant, trying to read the man's face. When the door closed behind them, the lieutenant broke into a smile.

"It's a match!"

Jason felt his heart begin pumping again. "Positive?"

"Definite. Both the slug and casings match. Also, they checked for fingerprints. Only one person's were found on the weapon."

"Our reporter friend's?"

"That's right."

The lieutenant, who had only known Vanessa a short time, laid his hands on Jason's shoulders. The emotion from Savage was both surprising and sincere. "Vanessa is innocent!"

Jason's eyes welled up, and as much as he wanted to pump his fists and celebrate, he had a task to finish first.

Savage nodded toward the interview room. "Now see if you can get a confession."

Jason turned and re-entered the room, forcing his expression to remain impassive. Returning to his chair, he kept his voice in a monotone.

"Now, where were we? Oh, yes. The gun. Why didn't you turn it over when I asked for it? Could it be because you knew it would match the murder weapon used on Rob Layne?"

Devin's shoulders sagged, but he remained mute.

"Come on, Devin. We're old buddies, right? That's the way you acted on the street, so why can't you confide in me now?"

Something on the floor had become riveting for Devin. He stared at the spot between his feet, his posture one of defeat.

Jason crossed his arms and cocked his head to one side. "Here's what I don't get. What did you think your son would say when he found out you took revenge on Vanessa?"

Devin's eyes flared. "My son is dead!"

Jason rocked backward, stunned by the revelation.

Tears welled up in Devin's eyes, and his lips quivered.

Jason found himself lost for words.

Does James blame Vanessa for his son's death? How could that be?

Devin was wiping at his eyes now, trying to stem the tears. "You didn't know that, did you?"

Jason shook his head. "Until recently, I didn't even know you had a son."

"That's right. His mother died during his birth, and I raised him alone."

It was Jason's turn to be silent.

Devin stood and moved to the far end of the room, wedging himself into a corner. It looked as if he was trying to hide his vulnerability. He stared at Jason.

"When Layne got detective over my Bobby, he was angry. He thought his career was stuck at SAPD and he'd never get the homicide detail he wanted. I urged him to be patient, but he didn't listen."

Devin wiped a sleeve across his face.

"He opted to sign on with the Dallas PD. In order to make the transfer, he had to go back on the streets as a patrol officer. Three months later, he was killed answering a domestic disturbance call."

Jason stared at the man, who seemed to be shrinking before Jason's eyes, and tried to make a cohesive picture out of the pieces suddenly laying on the floor.

"Why kill Rob Layne?"

"It was Vanessa's fault! If she hadn't played the female card, my Bobby would have gotten the job, and he'd be alive today!"

"But why Rob?"

"So she could feel the pain I live with every day."

Jason rubbed his eyes. It seemed so far-fetched, so unbelievable, yet the pieces fit. Still, something was still not right.

"Did you plan to frame Vanessa all along?"

He shook his head. "That was happenstance. I went to call 9-1-1 to report the killing, and I heard her car. I hung up and ducked out of the garage before she saw me. I was glad to blame her."

"Why would you call 9-1-1 on yourself?"

Devin stared at Jason, apparently surprised at his inability to understand.

"To be first on the story, of course."

Jason's stomach churned; he'd heard enough.

"Stand up and turn around, James. You're under arrest for the murder of Rob Layne…"

John C. Dalglish

Epilogue

Standing just outside the booking room, he waited with the little boy's hand in his. They'd watched through the glass as the boy's mother was being processed for release and set free. Out of the prison jumpsuit and back in her own clothing, she looked like her old self. Even her smile had been restored.

When the door finally opened, she surged through, her eyes overflowing.

Jason let go of Kasen's hand, and the boy leaped into his mother's arms. She squeezed him tight, smelling his hair and whispering into his ear.

He leaned away from her. "I missed you so much!"

She grinned. "I missed you more."

"Uh-uh."

"Did, too."

She let Kasen down, and Rachel took the boy's hand. "Come on, Buddy. Let's go get the car."

"Okay."

Vanessa turned to Jason, and her happy tears escalated into shuddering sobs. She stepped forward and wrapped her arms around him.

"Thank you, thank you, thank you."

Jason matched her tears with his own. "I'm just glad you're out of there."

She pulled back. "It's not something I'd like to go through again, that's for sure!"

"That makes two of us."

Sandy stepped out from behind her husband. "Make that three of us."

Vanessa hugged Sandy. "I can't say how much you two mean to me. I wouldn't have made it without you."

Sandy's eyes glistened. "I'm just glad it's over."

Jason looked at both women. "Let's celebrate! How does steaks on the grill sound?"

"Awesome!"

Rachel pulled up outside, and the group made their way into the fresh air. Vanessa inhaled deeply and attempted to compose herself.

Rachel rolled down the passenger window. "What's the plan?"

Vanessa opened the door and got inside. "Steaks at Jason's"

"Sounds great. Meet you there?"

Jason nodded. "See you then."

As the car pulled away, Sandy's hand slipped into his. "Come on, we have a celebration to organize."

****

Two hours later, they were on the back patio, Jason supervising the steaks on the grill. Vanessa, with Kasen in her lap, was telling her tale of life on the inside.

Torres had made it for the party, as had Lieutenant Savage. The others promised to come as soon as they could. When Captain Morris showed up, Jason waved at her with his barbeque tongs.

"Hey, Sarah."

"Hi, everyone."

"You're just in time for food."

"I can't stay, but thanks for the offer." She turned to Vanessa. "Have you got a minute?"

Vanessa's smile disappeared, and a cloud quickly descended on the gathering.

"Sure. Kasen, go sit with your aunt, okay?"

SHADOW OF DOUBT

Vanessa rose from her seat and followed the captain out to the front yard. Everyone else tried to keep up the light mood, despite the concern over what was taking place up front.

After just a few minutes, Vanessa returned. Jason noticed her smile had returned, as well.

She stepped to the middle of the patio and held her arms up in exaltation.

"I'm off suspension!"

A brief moment of silence was followed by an eruption of excitement. Sandy grabbed her glass.

"This deserves a toast! To Vanessa, welcome back among the free *and* the working!"

Glasses clinked as Jason loaded the steaks onto a platter.

"Let's eat!"

****

As the evening wore on, the crowd swelled with the arrival of Doc Davis and Josie, and even Mary Faldo made an appearance. But then, with midnight approaching, the party diminished to just a few. Jason found himself sitting out back alone.

Rob was still gone, and he'd have to deal with that, which he'd so far succeeded in avoiding. But at the same time, it was as if his partner had come back from the dead.

He sensed someone next to him and looked up to see Torres. "I guess I'm gonna leave."

He smiled up at her. "I'm glad you could come."

"It was my privilege."

She hesitated, looking down at him then off into the distance.

"What is it, Dianna?"

"It's…well…you never doubted Vanessa. On the other hand, I was certain she was guilty. Do you think she can forgive me?"

Jason spotted Vanessa standing in the doorway. "Why don't you ask her yourself?"

Dianna spun. "Oh, I didn't know…"

Vanessa's smile was warm. "It's okay, Dianna. You did your job, which is exactly what I would have done. Besides, I don't have any room in my heart for a grudge right now."

Dianna appeared near tears but gathered herself. "Thank you."

"I do have one request, though."

"What's that?"

Vanessa's face broke into a wide grin. "Can I have my partner back?"

Dianna laughed then rolled her eyes. "You bet! He's so high maintenance."

Vanessa laughed. "Yeah, but I'm used to it."

Jason unsuccessfully attempted to appear hurt. Torres laughed and headed for the gate. After she had gone, Vanessa sat down next to Jason.

"I wanted to say again how much I appreciated your faith in me."

"It wasn't just me. Sarah Morris was in your corner, too. She pushed me to continue on with the case, even after your arrest."

"I'll have to remember to thank her."

Jason stared at his wineglass. "I have a confession of my own."

"Oh? Do tell."

"There were times when I struggled with the same questions as everyone else."

"You mean whether I could have done it?"

Jason nodded, his eyes avoiding hers. She touched his arm.

"Jason?"

He looked up at her, and she beamed with a devilish grin.

"Perhaps it's best you don't piss me off then, huh?"

John C. Dalglish

He laughed robustly, letting the joy of the day's events take over.

"True story, sister! True story."

****

Get a *FREE* copy of the ebook

"WHERE'S MY SON?" Detective Jason Strong #1

Visit this link.
http://jcdalglish.webs.com/

****

AUTHOR'S NOTE

Number 15! I can't believe it!

I can never say thank you enough to all of you who write letters and reviews. Your confidence in me is what keeps me motivated.

Hopefully, the ending of SHADOW was a surprise. I guess we'll need to replace

SHADOW OF DOUBT

another character! As they say—life goes on—for our heroes and those around them, even if it's in my mind.

Thanks again for taking the time to read our books. It is our honor.

God Bless, John
I Jn 1:9

Cover by Beverly Dalglish
Edited by Jill Noelle-Noble
Proofreading by Robert Toohey

OTHER LINKS:
jdalglish7@gmail.com
https://www.facebook.com/DetectiveJasonStrong

Made in the USA
Columbia, SC
24 November 2020